The Spider

THE INDIA LIST

AURKO MAITRA

The Spider

Seagull Books

LONDON NEW YORK CALCUTTA

Seagull Books, 2025

First published by Seagull Books, 2025

ISBN 978 1 8030 9 477 9

British Library Cataloguing-in-Publication Data
A catalogue record for this book is available from the British Library

Typeset at Seagull Books, Calcutta, India

The Spider

1

Rahim was the son of Qadir, the Spider. He resembled his father the way he had been twelve years ago, before the Ghosh brothers dragged him out to the fields and broke him, back when the village girls would hide in the forest to watch him bathe by the lake at dawn. He stood waist deep in the water, tall, dark and broad shouldered, his chest scarred like an abattoir slab, his eyes still and grey, like winter mist pressed against glass. Balanced upon tiptoes, he clenched his stomach and bathed slowly, for he always knew when they were watching. Even now in the afternoons when their sons are gone, the widows quietly recollect the way he'd leave stolen poppies in their hair.

The oldest of three brothers, Rahim sometimes thought he could remember his father when he was younger. This memory of Qadir carrying him through the forest on his shoulders, in the flowering shadows of the crooked, bone-white mohuas, the ashen sals, the Spider humming so softly you could barely hear him over the sound of the river. It was the faintest of recollections. Perhaps something he'd seen in a dream, even. A half-forgotten cinema. This wasn't something he spoke of to his family, because he knew they'd just tell him he was too young to remember. It was how he learned to keep his phantoms close, to foster them in silence. What wasn't uttered could never be taken away.

Rahim's mother told him he had his fathers' flat nose and a strong ploughman's shoulders. The same carven cheekbones. The same fine, dark lips charred by smoke. How pink they'd once been, she said. It was known that he held in him his father's old laughter, his old lust, that he even mirrored Qadir's bygone stride, sleek and leonine. You could see it in the way his mother's eyes glazed over as she watched him eat. In the way she fed him more than her other children, ladling rice and beef and sabzi onto his plate as soon as he licked it clean. There was a time this made his brothers scream and cry, but now they knew to be quiet. These days his siblings ate with their heads bowed low as their mother stood over Rahim's shoulders, telling him stories of his father's old hunger.

After lunch, Rahim would crouch down from across Qadir in the afternoons, watching his father sitting cross-legged on the floor of the dark asbestos hut, cleaning out the barrel of his AK-47 as his mother wandered the room with a duster. As he worked, Qadir told stories of climbing the teak trees beyond the hills, the bolts and cartridges laid out across the thin rattan mat before him like a clockmaker's tools. Ever since he'd begun walking again, Qadir had gone back into his old line, killing for the Alams. Sometimes he still hummed as he cradled the rifle in his lap. His voice low and resonant, the only thing that had remained after he woke from the coma. It seemed as if he'd shrunk ever since his bones were broken. His body now curled inwards, the limbs a twisted ruin of sinew and veins, clustering like the roots of a cancerous grove.

Yet even now, they said, under fire he was unworldly. The villagers told Rahim that though his father's gnarled fingers could barely make a fist, bullets couldn't down him. Even when you shot him, he seemed to keep coming. His warped, shambling form lurching through the trees like a black widow, then dissipating once more into the wilds. Now they spoke of him as the Makorsha, the Spider. A ghost in the field.

2

By the time Rahim went into his father's line, two of the Ghosh brothers were dead. The last one a vegetable. Qadir had settled their debts to him and moved on to other feuds. They got about ten thousand for each freelance killing. Worked on retainer for the Alams and the other Syndicate men in the long, meandering gun battles along Berapur's outer dark. Rahim couldn't tell you how these feuds began. They just searched for the names they'd been given. Sometimes men from other lobbies, sometimes their own. All he knew was what his father told him—the fighting would go on for some time, calm, then begin again. The killings, the retaliations. Boys' games. In times of peace, he told his sons to expect this. It was as inevitable as the monsoon, the harvest, the sowing of the fields.

He was thirteen and he'd just begun following his father and the other men out past the rice paddies beyond the village. About two dozen of them in banyans or loose office shirts, rusted AKs slung over their shoulders, the older ones wading through the tall grass with their lungis hiked up to their knees. They were faceless in the half-light. A trail of bodies crossing the darkened fields—his father hobbling, the others following him in the languid, stalking gait of stray cats. In low tones, they muttered about smoke along the horizon, voices rising from a clearing in the forest. When gunfire broke out, they scattered across the field and began shooting into the trees. It would go on for what seemed like hours, bodies falling, corpses disappearing in the tall grass. From a distance, you could not discern the silhouettes of the children from the men.

Along the outskirts of the village, nights seemed endless, recurring. When the shooting ended, they found twenty-four bodies—eight of their own, sixteen of the anti-party's. As some of the men carried off their wounded, Rahim and the others wandered the forest, machetes and butchers' blades in hands, dragging the dead up by their hair to behead them. His father told him these men were rapists and thieves and they would not pass into another life. Rahim spoke but couldn't hear his own voice, his skull still ringing from gunfire as he walked over the corpses. It was slow, laborious work, hacking away at the necks of the bodies, cutting down into the sinew and the string. Men laughed as they kicked the heads across the dirt, pissed on them, dashed them against the stones and trees as if cracking open coconuts for their flesh.

Rahim did as they did. He walked the field, looking out for the slightest twitch, the faintest sign of breath. He searched their eyes but found nothing. As he carved into them, he could feel the blood soaking through his shirt, slick across his smooth, hairless chest—warm and then suddenly cool. He almost gagged and the vomit burnt in his throat. When his arm became dead weight, he looked up and saw his father, the Spider, bringing the blade down on the limbs of a gunman so close to death he could only whisper something unintelligible as he fell apart. He watched this for a few moments, then turned back to the body before him. He took deep breaths and tried working like his father, quiet, methodical, dismembering them with the calm of a burning monk.

3

They returned home with the bodies of their men. The dead hired guns they left behind in a warehouse to be burned or buried. They lined up their dead in a field for their families to collect. Afterwards, they cleaned themselves of blood by the lake and walked down to the pitch together, smelling of iron and cheap tulsi soap. Qadir sat down with the other men and passed a bottle of Old Monk around as one them crushed ganja on a crumpled Sai Baba calendar. Rahim and the younger boys had their own circle on the other side of the field, but he could hear his father's laughter, stark and almost mournful as a bloodless sun seeped into the pre-dawn skies. The younger boys would only start drinking and yelling after the men were gone, but for now they spoke of the killings.

'Fuck, I didn't think we'd lose Akhtar,' One of the boys said.

'I got the one who got him,' Rahim said, touching his heart, 'I saw it was him, and I got him. That fucking Bihari, Malik or whatever. I recognized that ratface when I got him. I caught him in the head, but they took the body when they were running.'

'What bara,' another kid said, a sixteen-year-old they called Baltu, 'better be sure. And if see the fucker tomorrow, then what?'

'Then I'll kill him again. Bara, I'll kill him as many times as it takes,' Rahim said, glancing towards the far side of the field to make sure his father wasn't watching as he lit a bidi and smoked it with his head down.

'Bara, you'll kill him a hundred times.'

'I'd be happy to, but the fucker is dead. I'll bet you fifty bucks we don't see him in the field again.'

'Fifty bucks, all right,' Baltu grunted, 'you'll kill him a thousand times, bara.'

'You won't see the fucker, I saw him go down—I'm telling you.'

Rahim waved the bidi as he spoke, only lowering it once more after glancing at his father's circle, where the men were beginning to rise to their feet. After a moment of hesitation, he said in a whisper, 'And if we do see him, though we won't see him—if we do see him, I swear on my mother I'll kill him again.'

He saw his father approaching them, the fringe of his lungi raised in one hand. Rahim killed the bidi in the dirt. The boys quiet as they waited for Qadir.

'Ay,' he shouted as he made his way over, then stood still and frowned as he sniffed the air stale with tobacco smoke. Rahim was about to say something, but Qadir stopped him.

'Don't be too late coming back,' his voice slurred with rum. 'Your mother's up waiting.'

'Yes, Baba,' Rahim said.

'We'll see you, Chacha,' the rest of the boys said in unison.

Qadir nodded at the boys and made his way back across the field towards the village. The boys didn't say anything until he disappeared into the trees, then brought out their own chillum, talking among themselves as Baltu crushed the ganja in his palm. Rahim watched as some of it slipped between his fingers onto the grass.

'Ay bokachoda, you're dropping it all over the place.'

'Fuck off, I'm not dropping anything,' he said, raising half his ass to fumble in his back pocket for his phone. 'Wait, bara, you know that girl Rania.'

Rahim grunted. He had some girls he spoke to, though it hadn't gone beyond that. Nothing worth talking about.

'You're dropping it,' he said. 'Stop crushing it. I'll get a base.'

'Listen na, bara, this girl Rania, she's been calling me.'

He got the phone out and began going through it.

'You're lying,' another boy said.

'Arrey bhai, she's sexy as anything,' said another.

'You're dropping everything,' Rahim said, leaning over to get a look at Baltu's phone.

'Ya, what am I saying?' Baltu said. 'And she wants to give out big time. She wants to meet.'

Rahim cut him off, 'Isn't her brother friends with Abdallah's guys?'

'So fucking what, take a look,' Baltu put the phone out, made sure everyone could see his WhatsApp record, which was a series of calls and emojis. 'Look at all the heart signs.'

'Oh shit,' the boys sounded off.

'Dhur, what would she want with your ugly ass.'

Baltu said, 'Ya, when I get a hold of that I'll fuck her like crazy.'

The boy grinning through this manic little shiver.

Rahim looked around at the boys, felt himself on the edge of saying something, but in the end, just stood up.

'Fuck it,' he finally said, 'you're dropping everything. I'll go find a base.'

'Where will you get a base now? Sit down, bara.'

'No matter where I'll find it, bara. Don't worry. I won't let you drop the maal everywhere. It's golden.'

He began making his way across the field towards where the older men had been sitting. His hands in his pockets as he kicked a rock across the ground. He looked out to the grass stretching towards the rail lines and the cluster of trees stirring in the southern wind like night birds, traces of dawn glinting in the dew. Almost certain the boys were watching him, he looked back over his shoulder, in anticipation. When he saw how they were all crowding over Baltu's phone, he turned back, watched for any signs of movement in the trees.

Then, as if satisfied, he kept walking. When he reached the spot where the men had been sitting, he could see bottles, chillums and bidi packets strewn across the grass, the crumpled page of a calendar lying among them. December 2021. A black-and-white picture of a garlanded Sai Baba sitting upon a stone, one palm raised. As he crouched to pick it up, he saw something in the ground beyond. His father's battle strategies carved into a grassless patch. Dusting off the calendar with one hand, he ran his eyes across the crude map—a circle drawn around a scatter of dots and crosses, like a game left behind by village children in the dirt. He could hear the boys shouting for him to return, but it only made him stay there longer, trying to decipher his father's markings. After a while he stood up slowly and nodded to himself as if he'd understood.

4

When Rahim asked his father how long their family had been in this line, killing for the Alams, Qadir had been quiet at first. It was something he would explain to the boy over years. What Rahim didn't realize was that for his father, to answer this was to answer how the sea began, the stars—to mark the birth of God, of shadows and the etchings in the banyans. In a way, it was almost beyond his conception. As if to imagine a time before time. He told Rahim they'd lived this way ever since anyone could remember. Their blood had soaked into the soil, and the soil belonged to the Alams. There is no reason we can understand, he said. All of this was written for us. All that we are, all that we will be, it is all written.

He heard stories from long ago, though he couldn't tell you from when. They had been spearmen in times of war. When peace came, they were guards, dacoits, overseeing the labourers in the sweltering poppy fields, dragging them out into the trees when they disobeyed the lord. Their violence had no claims to purity. They fought other men's battles, ploughed the fields of their masters. Ever since he was a boy, they told him his people killed so effortlessly because of their Bagdi blood, the way it was tainted, because it held the murky, ancient strain of some broken race that ruled these jungles long before history. It was his inheritance, they said—but he didn't know what to believe. Maybe it was just another ghost story.

Of course, there were many Bagdi boys who'd never gone into this line. Still, most became nothing more than farmers and labourers. Even then, even after all the men he'd killed for the Syndicate, his father couldn't pay for the surgeries to fix his bones, or wrench out the bullet that had been lodged above his belly for decades. They would salt the earth of a generation before they could move out of their rundown hut on the outskirts of town. When he was drunk on a big-money kill, Qadir would say it didn't matter, at least their work brought in fish and booze and meat and ganja— a name that couldn't be uttered around without a moment of silence, a glance over the shoulder. This is what he'd leave them.

These days they fed themselves off their boss's feud with the sons of Abdallah, a man his father had killed and desecrated on orders from the Alams. It was an act of justice, Qadir said. The man was a rapist and a thief, like all the others. By the time his boys came back years later to contest against the Alams in the local elections, it was something they'd all been waiting for. When they weren't killing in the fields, they were watching the horizon, biding their time for the return of brothers, of sons.

Rahim knew about the Ghosh brothers, but he didn't know how many others were out there searching for his father. After field training, he left home on a bicycle with a 9 mm down his jeans, knowing which paths not to take, the fields not to set foot in.

Throughout the day, Rahim and the boys rode the narrow, jagged path through the jungle, looking for a good spot. They left their bicycles and kicked off their slippers and climbed up the banyans. Cradled in the branches, they passed a bottle of Old Monk, their slender bodies marked by the flickering shadows of the leaves. Sometimes they heard the shrieking of animals as bombs went off in the distance, gunfire. It was enough to make them turn to each other, go quiet for a moment, a pause before they went on drinking. You could feel the blasts long after they were over. Their echoes pulsating in the calm, reverberating through wood and bone.

As the shots rang out, Rahim picked up insects from the leaves, scrolled through the photos they'd saved off the village WhatsApp groups. Always the same shit, he said—images of motorcycles, tholis fat with ganja. They sent bodies, severed hands, cough syrup and glamour shots of village girls. Dead fish and low-res porno. Chinese Kalashnikovs laid out on a faded-blue floral sheet. He raised the phone camera, did his hair a little, then flashed the pistol before snapping a photo for his background. Maybe something he'd send a couple of girls when he had data.

There were always killings, and rumours of killings. Amid all this, they wandered through the pitch, playing football or kicking stones across the dirt, looking for a buzz until something came along. A few of the boys did other jobs. Got just enough for a quick high in construction or driving trucks, working at all the paan shops and roadside stalls. Others made bombs down at the factory units on the outskirts of town. During breaks, they were back in the same fields, passing around chillums, waiting for the next call.

5

When Rahim and his brother worked, it was usually in the Alams' poppy fields, just as his father had done as a boy. He walked alongside the women and children through the farms, among the crops, the poppy flowers, scraping the clotted, wine-red milk from their heads with a curved blade. By now he'd stopped being conscious of the sentry towers. The cowled men guarding the perimeter with sten guns, watching them. On breaks he smoked bidis and roamed the fields, asking the older women for the names of the trees and flowers. He took his time, studying the ganja and poppies growing among the crops, sprouting between bean stalks and cabbage heads, their colours dulled by the wind and reddening dust.

He'd once heard his father say these fields were one of the reasons they were fighting. The Alams made crores pushing the product to backroom labs in Murshidabad, where it was processed into smack and trafficked across the borders. Out here it was dirt cheap and people began young. He was told it would be sold in the furthest reaches of the world, coursing beneath the vast, spectral skylines of cities beyond his imagination. He considered all this as he walked the fields, thinking of the pictures he'd seen of Dubai, Vancouver, London. With each poppy he cultivated, the curdled opium layered against his blade, its musk sweet and almost human.

He watched for snakes as he worked. Killed a mosquito on his neck, smeared its blood on his jeans. The hours seemed to draw out in the steaming heat, a slow, writhing languor. He peeled his shirt off with one hand and worked bare-chested, trying to catch the eyes of girls across the field. They always turned away, smiling if he was lucky, but sometimes he caught their mothers staring at him in a daze. Women who'd once known Qadir.

They were not like the younger girls, their eyes were unwavering. Once he'd heard the older men talk about how his father would bring them poppies from this very field. He could come up behind you, slip a flower into your hair without you knowing. The way the story is told, the moment the girl found out, the moment she brushed her hair with her fingers and grazed its petals, she would know she was chosen. Inevitably, she would follow him. Just like the others.

A lot was said of these women. Some told him there were no flowers. Just money. Others claimed it was his beauty that made them forsake their families and accept him as their one master, their one religion. They were nothing more than foolish young girls who'd been drawn to a wild and godless love, following

Qadir's gang out past the fields, two or three of them at a time, disappearing into the trees so he could have them all at once on the forest floor. It was said that when these girls lay in bed at night, beneath the squirming mass of their husbands, his name would always be at the cusp of their lips.

His father had told him he'd hear a lot of stories. These people will say anything.

6

By the time Rahim returned from the fields in the late afternoon, his father was sitting in the doorway of their hut, feeding a tethered calf hay from his palm. Party banners were strung above the corner shops. The name Alam was emblazoned across the boundary walls in washed-out blue.

The village roads were near-empty now and only a few older men lingered in the shade of a mango tree, smoking bidis as they talked about the next election. A small group of women whispered among themselves as they walked towards the well, pails swinging in their hands, laughter drawing the eyes from passing boys. It was coming to evening. His father looked up to see him approaching, but he turned away and continued feeding the calf. As Rahim came closer he could hear jackals from among the trees. The shrill call of brainfever birds ruptured the skies—a seeping hysteria.

'You haven't eaten all day,' his father said, straining to stand up as Rahim walked towards him.

'I ate at Sonu's house.'

'Don't tell your mother that,' Qadir grunted. 'She's been sitting there all day waiting to feed you. Give me the maal and go eat.'

Rahim passed him the pistol. His father tucked it into his lungi and covered the grip with his untucked shirt.

'You cleaned it?'

'Just this morning,' Rahim reached into the back pocket of his jeans, brought out the money he'd made from the fields. He tried to pass it over to Qadir, but his father didn't take it.

'Give it to your mother. It'll make her happy.' He waved Rahim away, 'Go. Go quickly and wash your hands and face and go eat.'

As he walked inside he could see his brothers sitting in one corner, watching videos on Qadir's phone. His mother, waiting for him on a mat across the room, touched his face as she took the money. She stood up and, without a word, walked over to the steel bowls of meat and dal and began preparing his plate.

'You must be starving.'

Rahim sat down in the centre of the room as he waited, ignoring his brothers when they called his name, told him to come watch something on the phone. He clicked his tongue at them. He didn't to say it again. Tell them how he was thirteen now and a real killer and he didn't have the time to watch their fuck-all clips of kids lip-syncing to Bollywood or whatever it was. When he got angry like this, they'd always turn to look at each other, giggling.

His mother laid out the food. Rice, cabbage and the two big chicken thighs she'd kept away from his brothers. He ate quickly and his mother watched him in silence. She piled rice onto his plate before he was done, brushed a grain off his chin. They could hear the voices coming from the phone. Ajay Devgn shooting off a one-liner from *Once Upon a Time in Mumbai—Zindagi ho toh smuggler jaisi, sari duniya raakh ki tarah neeche aur khud dhuen ke tarah upar*. Rahim recited it under his breath before it was over, even if he didn't quite know what it meant.

'What all you boys watch,' Rahim's mother said. 'They've been looking at those videos all day.'

'It's all trash,' Rahim shook his head.

'Oi,' one of his brothers said, 'don't talk like that. I know you watch them all night when everyone's sleeping. Along with all that other stuff.'

'Ay, I'll give you one behind the ear, you hear me,' Rahim said, raising a hand.

'Don't bother your brother,' his mother snapped. 'He's eating.'

Rahim stared at his brothers as he broke apart the chicken thigh with his teeth, figuring he'd get them later. Still, he couldn't push it too far. He was bigger than them and he could take them one-on-one, but they were all sons of Qadir. When it wasn't going their way they'd go for the balls and eyes. If they lost on a bad day they'd return half-conscious, slathered in blood with sickles in their hands, never knowing how much it was they truly wanted to hurt him. Once, when he was beating them two at a time, the third had come up from behind and downed him with a brick, only for them to howl and cry over his unconscious body when they thought he was dead. Qadir told their mother to leave them be. Just boys and their games, he said.

When he was done eating, he pushed the plate away, walked outside and washed his hands at the water pipe. Goats walked past, their heads swaying with each step. As the winds picked up, a haze of dust bronzed the leaves and battered the crops. The sky above was scorched white like steel in the forge. Beyond the water pipe, he could see his father hobbling waist high through their fields, the pistol dangling from his fingers as he inspected the paddy for weevils. He turned around at the emerging roar of an engine, his hand tightening around the grip of the 9 mm as he looked into the distance over Rahim's shoulder.

Rahim turned around and saw a motorcycle approaching them.

'Ay, how's it going?' a voice called out. As the bike came closer, they saw it was Baltu in track pants, flip flops and an Arsenal jersey, a bidi between his blackened lips.

Qadir walked out towards Rahim, the pistol still in his hand.

'Chacha, I hope you're well,' Baltu said, slowing the bike to stop beside them.

'Yeah, yeah—tell me, babu, what happened?'

'Nothing like that,' Baltu said, 'Some of us boys were just going to go swimming, figured I'd pick up Rahim.'

Rahim looked at his father, 'I'll go?'

'It'll be dark soon.'

'Arrey, Chacha, that's no problem, all the boys will be there. We'll come back together.'

Qadir considered this, nodding slowly—then he grunted and passed Rahim the pistol.

'Just don't be out too late. You know we've got work tomorrow.'

'All right.'

'And don't go into Ghatshila, they're killing our boys on sight out there,' he said, waving them off.

As Baltu fired up the bike engine, Qadir grinned and shouted over it, 'Or if you do, don't come back without a couple of heads.'

It was true what they said. Rahim and his father had the same laugh.

7

The bike gunned down a lone road cutting through jungles. Party flags were strung up above them. A haunted swathe of sal lead out to the borderland highways, towards Jharkhand. Clinging to Baltu, Rahim could see the smoke from the sponge-iron factory rising beyond the canopies, over the scattered villages and rice-wine shanties, little shades of bamboo and thatch strung together with scraggy jute rope, lean Adivasi women crouched beneath the tarpaulin, watching over steel vats of moonshine. Rumours of she-ghosts in the trees.

'We're going to meet Raniya,' Baltu shouted.

'Oh yeah?'

'She's bringing a friend, yeah. There'll be whiskey and all.'

Rahim felt a twinge in his stomach, 'Who's the friend?'

'I don't know, some cousin. She'll be sexy, bhai. All her friends are.'

Rahim forced a smile. Baltu turned the bike into a narrow path along the shoulder of the road.

'We loosen them up with a little booze, a little ganja—and they're all ours.'

They followed the dirt path deeper into the forest, where they found a small clay hut tucked among the sals, behind the murky grey waters of a rice paddy butchered by the monsoon storms. Clods of cow dung were pressed onto the walls, fingers imprinting them like the fossils of sea life or palmyra fronds.

Dogs ran out towards them and leapt up at their legs as they approached.

'Ay Mani-da,' Baltu shouted as he swung one leg back over his bike and held out his hand for the dogs to lick, 'You got it or what?'

After a few moments, a small, potbellied man stepped out of the doorway, one arm against the frame as he pushed himself forth, a half-empty bottle of whiskey tucked under the other. He was bare-chested with a piece of cloth draped over one shoulder. He was struggling to keep his lungi from slipping.

'Yeah, yeah got it,' he slurred, fumbling as he tried to pick up his bicycle, his hands all over the place.

'Oh dada, you've got it going already, haven't you?' Baltu laughed. Rahim stood behind him, playing with the dogs.

'Don't worry, I left that bottle for you,' Mani said, trying to lift the bicycle with one hand as he tried to hitch up his falling lungi with the other. 'You boys enjoy.'

'All right, all right.' As Baltu handed over a wad of cash, Mani dropped the bicycle to take it. Then, with no trace of a rush, he began the process all over again. The boys and the dogs stood and watched him pick up the bike and set off down the narrow dirt path—humming to himself between the swigs of whiskey.

'Old fucker is so drunk we're lucky there's anything left for us at all,' Baltu said as they stepped into the dark, dusty hut. 'But he's a good man. Lies like hell. Beats his wife like crazy. But he's a good man.'

The dogs stood at the doorway and stared. Rahim kissed one on the head before he sat down on the floor and began crushing a kali of ganja. Baltu walked over to one corner to grab the bottle of whiskey, which Mani had left on an upturned bucket, burning amber in a fading arc of sunlight. It was a small room, a thin mat was laid out on the floor. Empty plastic water jugs were stacked against one wall. A crude, black fish-scaling blade lay flat in one corner, its body glistening with the dull sheen of a python.

Baltu sat down across Rahim and placed the bottle between them. He brought out his phone and made a call. The girl picked up so quickly it made him wink.

'Hey,' he said, 'We're here, we've got the maal. Where are you? Your friend's coming, right?'

As Raniya begin to speak on the other end, he put a finger to his lip, whispered for Rahim to be quiet.

'I wasn't even saying anything, bara.'

Baltu cut the girl off after a few moments. 'What are you saying? We've got everything here, come on. You barely have to walk fifteen minutes. I even told you I can pick you up.'

Rahim lost the twinge in his stomach, realized it was one of those situations. The same thing always seemed to happen. Now he could drink without thinking.

'Come on, I'll pick you up. Just come.'

As he heard Baltu persist, he found himself pulling at strings in the mat.

'You're not coming? Fine.' Baltu hung up. 'Imagine, pagli wants us to go to some field in Radhanagar.'

'Radhanagar?'

'Ah fuck it—let's go.'

'Radhanagar. Yeah, we could go—but it's so far.'

'Let's go,' Baltu said, 'We can drink the two of us any day.'

Rahim thought about it for a moment. He didn't know what to say. He'd seen girls from afar, texted them—but when it came to seeing them face to face he had nothing .

Then, after some time, he got it.

'It's right by Ghatshila—Radhanagar.'

Baltu brought the bottle to his mouth and began gnawing at its seal, mumbling, 'That it is. Abdallah's got friends out there.'

'Her brother runs with them. What if it's a trap?'

Baltu slowly took a swig and scratched at a bleeding sore on his back shoulder as he considered this. Rahim watched him, his fingers searching for something to twist into, coiling the faint traces of hair on his legs. It took Baltu a few moments.

'Yeah, it's how they got Bikash-da, isn't it? Whore was trying to set us up.'

Rahim nodded his head slowly, 'It's how they get them in the movies too.'

Now certain that Baltu wouldn't take the risk, Rahim twisted his lips into that wicked smile he'd seen on Nawaz in *Psycho Raman*. 'Ay, I mean, we could go down get some maaggi anyway. Anyone comes I'm here.'

Rahim lifted his shirt, revealing the grip of the 9 mm.

'No, no, fuck it,' Baltu said, handing Rahim the bottle. 'It's my day off. I don't really feel like killing anyone right now.'

'All right, if you want.'

'We can just get high right here.'

They passed the bottle between them, taking swigs between puffs of the chillum, dragging it out so the booze and ganja could last till after dark. It was a hot evening, and Rahim could feel his eyelids growing heavy. He lit a bidi to keep himself awake. Rode out the long, dull high as he listened to Baltu going on about the girls he'd had out in the city.

They heard growling outside. The dogs scrambled by the doorway, their mangy white fur streaked in the billowing red dust. Rahim could never tell when they were playing.

He couldn't feel the minutes pass. He nodded at Baltu, drank, told him about the girls he'd had himself. All gone now, since they were just cousins passing through town. Family friends he'd snuck out with into the woods. So many that he couldn't remember their names. Or even if he did remember them, he wouldn't tell anyone because he wasn't one of those boys. Baltu talked over him, telling stories of Priya, whom he'd had out by the water pump, or Safia, in the cabbage field. They mumbled at each other this way for a while, names dissipating in the air.

'So I tell her,' Baltu says, 'I tell her, this is all it is right here. I don't have anything to give you. I've got baal to give you, understand?'

'I met a girl like that. Just wanted to be friends in the beginning. I'm like, I've got lots of friends. But I say okay and end up screwing her anyway. Then she wants more, and I get out quick. I don't want . . . wait a minute—' Rahim's head perked up. 'You hear that?'

'What?'

'Voices.'

Baltu frowned and sat still, listening. They could hear the voices of a man and woman slowly coming closer. Low tones in the quiet mania of the forest, undercurrents to the rambling bird calls. The rustling in the trees. Rahim was the first to stand up and walk slowly to the doorway, his fingers grazing the grip of the 9 mm.

'We should take the train out tonight,' the man said. 'This place isn't right.'

'We'll leave in the morning,' said the woman.

Rahim stepped out of the doorway, Baltu following behind. He could see their figures, adorned in white, gliding through the sals like lost spirits, reappearing beyond a veil of foliage. As they drew closer, Rahim began to discern one from the other. A squat, bearded man in malas and a pristine white kurta, a wooden string instrument tucked into one arm. A woman behind him, tall and stately with malas draped over her sari, her hair coiled in long, black dreads that almost brushed the forest floor as she walked.

'Musicians,' Baltu smiled at Rahim.

They seemed to have seen the boys, but their expressions did not change. They just seemed to go a little quiet. Rahim could just about make out their whispers as they came closer.

'Come,' the woman told the man. 'Don't worry. They're just boys.'

'You don't know the boys around here.'

Baltu stepped forward, smiled, 'Salaam alaikum.'

The man and the woman nodded in acknowledgement.

'Alaikum salaam.'

'That's a dotara, isn't it?' Baltu said, pointing at the instrument in the man's hand.

'Yes.'

'Where are you going?'

'Towards Berapur,' the man said.

'Nowhere,' said the woman.

'Come, sit,' Baltu said, 'play something for us.'

The man looked at the woman, who gave the boys a faint smile.

'We have ganja,' Baltu went on, pointing at Mani's hut. 'Come, sit, smoke. Sing us a song.'

'We should be moving on.'

'It's getting dark,' Baltu stepped forth and the man hesitated. 'Where will you stay tonight? You can even sleep here. We have ganja and all. Sing us a song, why don't you.'

The woman's smile widened. She touched the man's arm, gently guiding him forward.

'Come. Take us to your thek. We'll sing you a song or two.'

The musicians followed the boys down towards the hut. After Rahim and Baltu chased off the dogs, they brought out a chillum and laid the mat by the doorway. The four of them sat cross-legged, passing the clay pipe around as the man tuned the strings of his dotara, twin trails of smoke emerging from his nostrils like white mangrove roots. The woman sat straight up, one leg folded over the other, her hands upon her knees as though she were a dancer or a holy man.

'I'm Baltu, this is Rahim.'

Rahim nodded at the woman, whose eyes were fixated on his. She was taller than him, with hard, graven features. Dark circles rimmed her light-brown eyes, one of them misted a visceral red, a collapsed vessel blossoming around one pupil—clouds tinged with sunrise.

'Amira,' she said after a while. 'This is Salim.'

The man nodded at them.

'Where do you come from?' Baltu passed the chillum to the woman.

'I'm from Chandernagore.' She raised the pipe to her lips and took a drag. It was the first time Rahim had seen a woman smoke a chillum.

'Rajshahi,' Salim said.

Baltu grinned. 'That's in Bangladesh, isn't it?'

Salim nodded.

'You hopped a fence to get here, didn't you?'

'Tell me,' Salim ignored him, 'what do you boys do?'

'We work,' Baltu said.

'For the party?'

'Everyone works for the party,' Rahim cut in, speaking to them for the first time.

'I suppose you could say that,' the woman said as she lowered the chillum, waiting a few moments as they all fell silent. Then: 'Salim, you're ready? Shall we sing?'

Salim took the chillum in his hand, had one last drag before he propped up the dotara in his arms and prepared to play.

'Let's begin.'

Amira nodded at him, took a breath and tapped her fingers on her knee as she began. Rahim played with the grass as he listened, trying to make out the words from her long, drawn-out howl, her palm rising slowly, her voice as strong and clarion as coastal bells.

'*Oh you come to me this dusk, this long and endless dusk,*' she sang, her voice humming through the dirt. '*Oh you come to me and lay down a sheet bearing gifts, bearing trinkets.*'

Salim played with his eyes closed, his long, bony fingers crawling like a spider along the neck of the dotara.

'*Oh you come to me this long, endless dusk along the highway, you lay down a silk sheet bearing gifts, bearing trinkets, your gemstones remnants of the sun.*'

Her voice rose gradually, becoming its own entity, a creature walking among them.

'*Oh, you bear gifts, you bear trinkets, you bear hearts of clay. The shattered remnants of the sun hang off your golden chains.*'

The dogs seemed drawn towards them, ambling slowly from around the trees. Baltu took a swipe at them and went back to watching the woman, his eyes wide and glinting. Rahim let his shoulders slump and listened.

'*Oh, you came to us at dusk. This endless dusk with your gifts and trinkets. With your hearts of clay, shaped with small hands in the bygone river, left to harden in the bygone sun. Oh, you bear hearts of clay. Shaped in the ghost of the river, hardened in the sun you promise us.*'

Whatever they did, the dogs seemed to return, huddling around their circle. As Baltu raised his arm once more, Amira spoke softly between the verses.

'Leave them be, babu. Of course they will come,' she said, her voice suddenly magnifying as she continued the song. '*Oh, you with your promises of dawn, you speak too sweetly. You speak too sweetly.'*

The dogs clambered around, staring with blank eyes. Baltu kept turning back over his shoulder to keep watch.

'*Oh, you with your promises of dawn. You speak so sweetly. Too sweetly. You burn our possessions, only to name your pyre daylight. Oh, the daylight you promise us. You who comes bearing gifts, bearing trinkets—bearing your hearts of clay. You name your pyre daylight.*'

When she finished, she sat with her head bowed as Salim continued, his head swaying with the music. Looking at her, Baltu shuffled a little closer and passed her the chillum. She nodded, raised it to her lips as Baltu lit a match, lowering the flame to the mouth of the pipe while she took a drag. Rahim stared at the floor and waited until Salim had finished to ask her, 'What was that song?'

'I haven't given it a name yet.'

'You wrote it?'

'Yes.'

'So what does it mean?'

She blew out smoke through her lips. 'You tell me.'

Rahim forced a laugh as he took the chillum from her.

Baltu leaned back propped himself up on one arm, waving a bidi in his fingers as he spoke: 'It's about the party, isn't it?'

Amira turned to look at him but didn't say anything. Salim leaned back, gently plucking the dotara after long moments of silence, the notes lingering among them.

'Oh I know all about that,' Baltu went on. 'You stay around here, you'll know that. Party fucked this place to death with promises.'

'It's everywhere,' the woman said.

'Oh yeah, it's everywhere, it's everywhere. They're all the same. Look at this place—this is not a good place. You're lucky it was us you came across.'

Rahim tried to give him a look, a sign to quiet down, but Baltu had whiskey in him and all he saw now was Amira.

'Oh, you're lucky. You don't know how lucky you are.'

Salim held the dotara a little closer to his chest, a hand resting on the strings to keep them still. He was sweating through his kurta. Baltu turned to him, raised his eyebrows and said, 'What, Dada? You know how lucky you are? You don't, but there are a lot of bad people around here who could do all kinds of things to you.'

Salim didn't respond, but his face was hardening. Rahim had seen it before. Men and their masks.

'You're travelling around here with a woman like this. You know all kinds of things happen out here.'

'I can handle myself,' Amira said.

'But you've met us. And we're good boys, but we can also be not so good. You get any trouble, you just call me. We don't let that shit happen around here. We'll chop the fuckers piece-piece and toss them real quick.'

'How old are you?'

'What does that matter?' Baltu slapped Rahim on the back, 'See this boy right here? Just a little boy, right? Well, the little fucker's a killer. A crazy fucker.'

The woman smiled, brushed her locks back to get a good look at the boy. Rahim met her eyes, then quickly turned away, scowling at Baltu.

'Come on, Rahim, show them the machine.'

'He's joking.'

Salim tried to get Amira's attention with a jerk of his chin, signalling that they should leave, but she ignored him.

'Tell me, babu, how many people have you killed?'

Rahim looked at the ground.

'What did you kill them for?'

'It's in his blood, that's what for,' Baltu said, smiling. 'You want anyone dead, his family will do it. His father, uncles, everybody. They'll do anything.'

'But why?'

Noticing the way the woman was watching him, Rahim hesitated for a moment, then finally spoke up, 'Because that's what we do, we watch out for the people around here. Lots of bad people around here.'

'Do you know the people you kill?' Amira's voice was cheerily singsong, the way you speak to a child.

'Not usually,' Baltu said. 'We go after whoever they tell us to. That's just how it is.'

'And they pay you?'

'Why else?' Baltu raised his hand, 'Come on, Rahim, show the machine na.'

Rahim glanced around the circle, then leaned back and raised his shirt, revealing the grip of the 9 mm pressed against his flat stomach. Emboldened by the fascination in Amara's eyes, he drew the gun and held it out for them to see. Baltu began laughing.

'And you've used that before?'

Rahim tried to give her a knowing smirk, but ended up giggling instead. Amira nodded. Salim, his eyes fixed on the gun, seemed to relax at the sound of Rahim's laughter.

After a long pause, Salim stared ahead and spoke, 'You know, this was all written fourteen hundred year ago.'

'What was?'

'It was predicted in a hadith. It was said the killed will not know who killed him, and the killer will not know who he has killed. Fourteen hundred years ago this was written.'

Rahim leaned in to listen.

'And before that, the great Vedic astronomers had the same claim. They said this was the Kali Yuga, the blind age.'

'What are you talking about?' Baltu said.

Salim ignored him, continuing as though he hadn't heard the boy.

'It is said it began five thousand years ago, the day Krishna left the earth. It was all foreseen. All of this is already written.'

'What did it say?'

Salim paused for a moment, cleared his throat.

'It said that servants will have no reason to trust their masters, nor masters their servants. The oceans will become barren. The cities shall be ruled by thieves. It was all written. Man's consciousness shall shrivel. We will not recognize our mothers. We will forget God, become creatures of blindness, numb to everything but hunger, with no idea why we're killing and dying.'

Rahim, suddenly feeling nauseous, denied the chillum when it was passed to him. He was thinking of the field now. The way they fired into the trees.

'With all due respect, Salim-da,' Amira began, 'and with respect to the holy men and their scriptures—haven't we always lived this way?'

'Perhaps.'

'We've always been like this. Have we not always walked into the unknown, conquering tribes, creating empires out of this blindness? To romanticize a past we will never fully know or understand—it's little more than a comfort.'

Salim smiled faintly, put the dotara down in his lap while stroking one of the dogs with his other hand. Baltu shuffled even closer to the woman, muttering something Rahim couldn't hear. He thought about moving towards them, but he didn't, he just sat there crushing more ganja for the chillum—her words coming to him all at once. A babel of nightbirds.

'So when is it supposed to end?' Rahim finally asked.

'What?' Salim said.

'This blind age, how long is it?'

'About four hundred thousand years from now, upon the arrival of Satya Yuga. The age of enlightenment.'

'It's taking its sweet time,' Baltu said. 'It's the local train or what, bara?'

Four hundred thousand years. To Rahim, for whom each endless, sweltering stretch of summer was an aeon, this number was little more than an abstraction. In his head he tried to give it a sense of form, but it remained shapeless, out of reach. He saw his mother holding his children. His father's funeral, the broken body draped in white silk and jasmine. He saw his brothers as men. Tall and unrecognizable with rifles cradled in their arms, following him out into the trees after dark. Four hundred thousand summers. Four hundred thousand years of blindness.

'Why don't you tell me something,' Amira leaned over, speaking to Baltu in a whisper meant for all of them. 'How many people have you killed?'

It was the question Baltu had been waiting for. Still, he played his part, staring off into dead space while muttering to himself, pretending to count on his fingers.

'Enough that I can't keep count any more.'

'Really?' Amira sounded delighted.

Rahim rolled his eyes, but Amira didn't seem to notice him.

Baltu, however, did. He tried drawing the story back, knowing Rahim would sell him out the moment he pushed it too far.

'But that's nothing out here,' he went on. 'There are guys out here who kill every week, every other day sometimes—a lot of them can't keep count.'

Salim seemed to have lost interest, he'd gone back to tuning the dotara, waiting until Amira was done with the conversation. She sat there beside the boy, wide-eyed.

'We have a dada out here,' Baltu continued. 'He'd gone to buy fish when he came across some anti-party fucker on the way. Chopped up the fucker right then and did the groceries after.'

He hadn't said it, but Rahim knew Baltu had his father in mind, though the story wasn't quite right. Qadir hadn't gone to the market. It had been a trip to the barber.

'And when you killed someone,' Amira motioned to Baltu to pass her the chillum, 'what was it like? How did it feel?'

'Sometimes it's like scoring a goal in football,' he winked. 'Sometimes like sex.'

'You don't mean that,' she said. The boys saw a challenge.

'It's better than sex. At its worst, it's just work. Like killing flies or ploughing the fields. You do it without thinking too much. All you think about is the way to get it done.'

Like ploughing the fields. Rahim scoffed, knowing Baltu was talking about depths he'd never reached. He could have told them about the first man he'd killed. A scrap dealer he'd put down on his knees and executed in Bokaro. His father had stood behind him, telling him to take a long, deep breath as he squeezed the trigger. He didn't see it happen. Nor can he remember the shot.

All he knows is he did what he was told and he heard the crying stop. Next time don't close your eyes, his father had told him as they walked home through the forest. Don't look away.

'It's easier for some people than others,' Rahim said after a while. Baltu had been gradually shifting closer to Amira as their conversation went on. He now sat almost shoulder to shoulder with her. She didn't move away, as though she hadn't noticed. Rahim considered speaking up to tell her Baltu was lying—he couldn't slaughter a goat. Instead, he just ended up repeating himself.

'I said it's easier for some people than others.'

Again, only Salim was listening, though he had no response. Their eyes met briefly before both looked away—the musician plucking his dotara, the boy pretending to go through his phone. Lighting a bidi, Rahim scrolled through photos of girls, angling the screen towards Baltu and Amira, hoping she would ask who they were. Salim noticed, but he simply plucked his strings and hummed. The dogs slowly ambled towards him, watching him with beady black eyes.

'But you know, whatever I've done, as long as you don't make me angry, I'm a good guy,' they all heard Baltu tell her. 'Ask the women around here. They'll tell you I'm not like the others. Not at all.'

8

There was another story Rahim had heard about his father. A month after Qadir began walking again, he'd been sipping tea in the market when he saw one of the Ghosh brothers down the street getting his phone recharged at the mobile shop. The man walked by Rahim's father but didn't recognize him. Qadir hadn't left home in years. Now a bearded, greying cripple sitting in the market, he might have been mistaken for a baba—a Sufi mendicant seeking alms.

He waited there for a while, taking the time to finish his tea as he watched the man standing by the shop, picking his nose. Qadir looked around on the streets for anything he could find, anything that would feel good in his hand. A brick, ideally a rod. He decided on a broken water pipe lying on the road. After paying the tea seller his five rupees, he began limping towards the cigarette shop, reaching down effortlessly to pick up the pipe along the way. An old grace you no longer saw except in his acts of violence.

Coming up behind Ghosh, Qadir paused, as if waiting for something. Then, just as the man began to turn, he swung the pipe against his skull. When he dropped his head cracked against the concrete and his body jerked and shuddered as Qadir stood over him. Clubbing him over and over, one hand tugging at his own slipping lungi, baring his thin, ashy legs. A crowd gathered but no one did anything. He kept going until the adrenaline died and the pipe felt heavy in his hands. By the time he was done, he could hear the soft whistle of Ghosh's breath wheezing through his broken oesophagus, his head split open and dribbling onto the concrete.

'Your father caught him just like that,' an uncle had told Rahim a year later. 'Afterwards, we came down and helped him load that fucker onto the back of a construction truck. Dumped him outside his boss's place. Told them we came to return his dog.'

Rahim had grown up with these stories, but they were different each time. The fragments of his father's shattered, ever-mercurial history. A thread of silk in the indecipherable web of rapes, killings and reprisals that had slowly entwined over the years. Not a war, nor a revolution, but an entity unto itself. The greater vendettas subsuming the lesser, breeding across the countryside like locusts in the plains. This was the grand design of their lives. Qadir never told his sons what he'd passed down to them. He was told he would be remembered, but a part of him knew his story wouldn't find peace in death. It would be re-envisioned under a shifting balance of power, transcending to the grotesque and the heroic, only becoming vaguer over time. The gunman slowly dissolving into myth, into oblivion.

'Don't listen to a word of it,' Qadir had once told Rahim as they practised shooting by the rice paddies. Crouched behind Rahim, he guided the boy's hands along the grooves and etchings of the rifle, directing it towards the Limca bottle sitting on the rickety wooden fence.

'People talk a lot of shit, and you'll never really know what's true.'

When Rahim's hands were in place, Qadir slowly released them.

'Now relax. Forget everything. All you need to know of this world is right down that barrel.'

This was the certainty he was given. Say your prayers, but know that out in the field you will not see God. There will be nothing but your hands and your tools and the soil beneath you. The future is meaningless, he was told. You can't even trust tomorrow. Just take a long, deep breath as you squeeze the trigger. See how the bursting glass catches daylight, like broken remnants of the sun.

He listened. He always listened. It was in his father's words that the world came into being. As Rahim and his brothers followed Qadir through the jungles and the rice paddies, he would tell them to look closer. This was the world they were fighting for, and it wouldn't be here much longer. Taking the diseased rice plants in his hands, he taught them this was not decay, but regeneration. This was the way life emerged, feeding on what came before it. Scarring the leaves and baring them of colour.

He told them that when city people came to the jungles, they saw chaos. But Qadir walked among ancient cities of canopies and blossoming vines. He showed them the arjuns and pigeonwoods, the sacred, primordial groves that had once been worshipped as shrines. Bulbul nests lay in the crooks of date palms. Mosquitos seethed in the core of a ripened jackfruit, feeding, their black bodies smeared with its reeking yellow pulp.

This is what you needed to know, not the past or future, but the blight, the fruit flies, the amaltas. The poison roots clawing from the dirt. One day, he told his sons, this too will be razed. Still, they must master this forest. Only then will they have the right to plough their fields from its ashes, tend to their stalks and take up arms when the time comes. If they are good to it, it will thrive in the monsoons—each harvest a quiet slaughter. They will not know hunger, he promised. These lands will be stark and golden. They will sow their seeds and bring it all under their order.

'That's what will happen,' he said, leading them out beneath the trees. 'People will think of these jungles and say there was nothing out here. The farmlands will come, and then they will be buried beneath the homes and the factories. Then the offices will come and the cities will bury them all.'

This was the only reason he could still find to talk to his eldest son: politics and cultivation—protecting the turf, cleaning their weapons and preparing for war. He was different with his other children. He laughed with them about football or cricket, looked over their games of PubG with a bemused fascination. With his wife and eldest son, he was quieter. Rahim would spend entire days with his father, cutting stalks or thinning out the seedlings in the paddy, oiling firearms on the mat, Qadir's orders cutting through the long stretches of silence between them. On the rare occasion Qadir ran a hand through his son's hair, he'd notice how the boy would try not to smile too wide, and he'd end up smiling too.

It was something his mother had only spoken of only once, on a day when Rahim was home alone with her, sitting across from her as she ground chilies with a mortar and pestle. The boy fanning her with a folded newspaper to break through the moist summer heat.

'Oh, don't even talk about your father,' She said, 'You were so young when it happened. You don't know him any other way.'

Rahim looked up at her.

'By the time you were walking he was still in bed. He couldn't even carry you around anymore. He was always whining to me, telling me I can't do this, I can't do that. What could I say? He'd tell me: I'm waiting in bed as the men go fight, like a woman.'

Rahim kept waving the newspaper, but it didn't seem to do much. His mother used the sharp, bony edge of her palm to skim the sweat off his glistening forehead, flicking it off her fingers before she went back to grinding the chilli powder.

'Since then, he's never been the same with us. Why? Because we had to take care of him. We had to bathe him. We had to take him to the bathroom and clean him.'

'Yes.'

'You were the one who would help me. Your brothers were so young.'

Rahim didn't respond, but he remembered those days. He'd grown up doing the groceries. He'd taken Qadir to the bathroom and cleaned him. Another memory. His father lying half-naked in the corner of the cool, dark room, his mother washing him with a dish cloth, soaking it in a bucket of lukewarm water before patting his chest. Qadir's body tensed. His glassy eyes flitting away from hers, like a trussed-up boar avoiding the gaze of its hunter. Rahim's mother worked without expression. It happened so quietly he hadn't noticed at first. He saw his mother had taken his father's head in one hand and made him look at her, even as his neck tightened, his body shuddered. She held his head still and stared him down as she bathed him. She made him watch.

It was something they would all pretend to forget over time. When Qadir began walking again, Rahim expected him to remember everything. He anticipated the day his father would raise a hand and strike his mother in return, just so he had a reason to fight the man, though he couldn't tell you why. It was something he would never tell anyone. Qadir was broken now and it would be easy to put him down. Still, Rahim didn't end up hitting his father, nor did his father ever strike his wife for what she'd done, or even speak of it. It was just that Qadir could never quite look her in the eye again.

9

They'd lost forty-four more men by midsummer. Eight of them missing. The rest found along the fields and the highways, some headless, others blinded and castrated, dismembered and dumped into mass graves. Their limbs strung up in black trash bags for their families to find among the trees. Rahim always thought about how villagers mourned over whatever remained. He had once seen a crying woman clutch a severed finger to her chest, howling at the men who tried to take it from her, promising them it was her son.

The eldest of the Alam brothers, Mustaque, arrived in the village after another funeral. It was the day the villagers were mourning one of his battalion leaders, gunned down outside a Berapur garage. About sixty of them were waiting outside the Masjid to receive him. Rahim stood beside his father. Both of them in crisp, white kurtas sharp with attar. Qadir reached out to touch his son's shoulder as Alam's sleek, black Scorpio cruised beneath the sal trees towards them.

You could see the darkened reflection of the leaves on the enamel, sweeping across its hood like rain. Rahim narrowed his eyes but there was nothing behind the tinted windows. As the car slowed down past the stunted huts and stopped by the Masjid, the crowd seemed drawn towards it, slowly encircling the Scorpio like it was a shrine.

Mustaque stepped out slowly, his black boots imprinted in the swirling red dust. He waved to the crowd as he heaved himself out of the car. A tall, big-bellied man with gold chains and ringed fingers, a white khadi kurta with wayfarer shades dangling from the collar. He smiled at the villagers, a hand upon his heart. Gave Qadir a quick nod before addressing the crowd.

'We lost a good man today. Oh, Rahul, they took you so young.'

His bodyguards had followed him out of the car, city boys from Calcutta and Banaras. All disco shirts and white tennis shoes, 9 mm's shoved down the backs of their ripped Affliction jeans. They stood back as Mustaque approached the crying women in the crowd.

'Didi, how could this have happened?' Mustaque spoke to the oldest among them, the battalion leader's mother, his arms stretched out as if she could answer his question. 'Like my own son, I loved him—I did. How could this have happened?'

As he spoke, the crowd seemed to close in. A swarm of white. It was only the mother who didn't seem to notice him. The words hadn't come to her yet. Her eyes were still swollen from crying.

'Oh, what can I tell you, Didi? What you have suffered, there is perhaps nothing worse in this life.'

The woman covered her face with her shawl, turned away. Rahim saw how she clenched the fabric in her fist.

'Of course you shall be looked after.' Mustaque turned to one of the city boys and switched to Hindi, 'See that she wants for nothing.'

'Ji, Bhai,' The gunman nodded, his hands folded in front of him.

The woman looked at the politician, her eyes suddenly glaring and white hot, 'You'll pay me for his life, is it?'

Women's hands reached out from the crowd to touch her shoulder, as if to calm her, but she went on.

'If all you have for us is money, then my daughters, my grandchildren—I'll let them starve. I don't want your money.'

Shaking his head slowly, Mustaque said, 'Then you want justice. You'll have that too.'

The mother burst into tears. The women stroked her back, muttered to her over her shoulder.

'We will bring you justice,' he said, summoning Qadir with a flick of his wrist.

Rahim watched his father approach Mustaque, who gripped Qadir by his shoulders and looked him in the eye.

'Qadir, you will find these miscreants, won't you? You'll get this poor woman her retribution.'

'Of course, Mustaque-da. Of course,' he pounded his chest, making a sound like a hollow oak. 'I won't let these dacoits walk.'

Mustaque squeezed Qadir's shoulders, then looked at the woman: 'None of us will.'

Rahim saw how his father stood waiting with a faint, child-like smile as Mustaque towered over him. He just about grazed the politician's shoulder, then let his hand fall limp to the side. The two city boys came and flanked Mustaque as he began to walk ahead, shepherding the mourners towards the Masjid.

Qadir waved at Rahim to follow, but he didn't go with his father. He stood and watched the women who stayed back as the men began to leave, gathering around the dead man's mother, holding her as she stumbled forward, collapsing into their arms. She was trying to scream but she couldn't. As her shawl slipped to the ground, Rahim could see her face was petrified in a long, silent wail that just wouldn't come. A woman picked it up for her, and it was only after a moment did Rahim realize it was his mother. She held the crying woman by her waist, whispered in her ear, wiped the sweat and tears from her cheeks.

He didn't move, hoping his mother would call his name, or at least look at him. A part of him thought she would call him over. Make him swear upon her soul to avenge this woman, perhaps, or even to walk her and her daughters home safe. But nothing was asked of him. The women just held her, some of them crying with her, carrying her forth one step at a time. For a moment his mother glanced at him, then looked away. He waited a moment longer, but when nothing came, he turned around and walked towards his father. After a while he broke into a slow jog, then a run, as if he was trying to catch up with the other men. It was as though his mother hadn't seen him at all.

10

After the funeral, Rahim was sitting with Baltu and the other boys outside the Masjid, waiting for their next chance to smoke a bidi in the mango orchard. It was late noon and most of the local shops were shuttered. A lone vendor waited for the mourners outside. The scent of hot milk and tea leaves roiling in the humid air. Rahim put a hand on the breast pocket of his kurta to check for his matchbox, and a passing mourner touched his heart and said salaam in return.

Rahim nodded at the man, then turned to the boys, smiling at himself.

'What's so funny?' One of them asked.

'Nothing,' he said.

He looked out to the crowds and saw his father coming towards him, limping over as quickly as he could.

'Ay, Rahim, come here.'

'Yeah, Baba,' Rahim said, motioning to the boys that he had to leave.

As the old man came closer, Rahim could see he was smiling.

'Go start up the bike,' he said. 'Your Mustaque-chacha said he wanted to see you.'

'Really?'

Mustaque Alam hadn't said anything to him at the funeral. He hadn't even looked his way.

'Hurry up, na.'

'Coming, Baba,' Rahim turned to the other boys and winked.

Rahim had never been to the Alam house before. Deep in the back of his mind, a part of him was convinced the politician would ask him to take over as battalion leader, something he felt he could draw into reality with sheer will. He drove down towards the estate on an ice-blue Yamaha, his father sitting behind him, a hand resting upon each knee.

They didn't speak as they coursed along the narrow forest roads. You could hear the tribes of grey langurs in the trees, their howls lingering across the sky. He drove with his chest pumped up, often glancing back to catch Qadir's eye, making certain his father was watching him. When the wind stopped, he felt the choking heat and revved the engine, gunning it just so he could breathe. A solitary breeze carried the smell of cool soil, amaranths and rotting vines. A decay bred into the earth.

'Your Mustaque-chacha said the men were all talking about you,' Qadir shouted over the roaring engine.

Rahim stared ahead as his father put a hand over his shoulder, making sure Qadir didn't see his cheeks flush.

'They were saying you shoot like a cinema hero,' Qadir laughed. 'That you'll shoot better than me one day.'

There was a faint chuckle from Rahim. As they came closer to the Alam house, the birds seemed quieter. They could see the narrow paths through the forests, leading into the processing labs, arms units and the poppy fields beyond them. Sentry towers lurked among the sweep of the canopies, masked men stood watching them from above, their bright-red bandanas flickering through the leaves like jasmines.

They could see the estate through the trees. A vast, palatial mansion with skyvines draped upon its faded, moss-grown walls, twining the intricate, floral grilles of the verandas and louvered windows. Ivies petrified in black iron. Rahim drove down the small dirt path that led to the walled-off gardens. Two skinny Adivasi boys stood by the entrance in jeans and battered slippers, AKs resting in the crooks of their arms.

Qadir raised a hand as the bike approached the Alam house. The Adivasis nodded as they came closer, opened the large sheet-iron gates lined with party flags. They nodded to Qadir as the bike passed through.

'Now tell me if you've ever seen a place like this,' Qadir grinned, leaning over Rahim's shoulders to see his eyes light up.

Rahim guided the bike along a dusty red-brick path that divided the sprawling English lawn. Past the tall, shining marble fountain, you could see the Alam children playing a game of cricket. Boys his age, he thought. An old man and his young son walked across the cropped grass in their lungis, tending to the sunken gardens of zinnias, pale balsams and black-eyed Susans. A few of Alam's gunmen watched the game from beneath the shade of the palash trees, dazed on opium as they smoked bidis and played cards on the grass.

'This belonged to the sahibs, once,' was all Qadir said.

They entered the estate through the servant's door. Qadir led his son down the wide, enamelled corridor into the drawing room, where Mustaque Alam was waiting. Still in his mourner's clothes, the politician lay on a fainting chair with a cigarette between his fingers, the other hand in a bowl of roasted nuts, his body spread-eagled beneath a gallery of mounted deer heads and vast, swirling oil canvases. Depictions of the forest. A Royal Bengal tiger stretched across the wall in rich safflower, a hunter among the trees, stalking its prey across the faux marble walls. Rahim stared at them, his jaw going a little slack. The smell of incense and crumbling books lingered in the dust.

Alam sat up and waved over Qadir and his son.

'Qadir, salaam alaikum. Come . . .'

'Walaikum salaam,' Rahim and Qadir responded, standing before him, waiting.

'Look at your son,' Alam said. 'He looks just like you.'

Qadir touched his heart.

'So this is the little boy who's got all the bastards in Berapur running.'

Rahim smiled and nodded.

'Good, good,' Mustaque said, then shouted across the room, 'Oh Kamala, bring two chairs and some fresh lime sodas.'

He turned to Qadir, 'Who can have tea in this heat, no?'

Then looked at Rahim, winked.

'Absolutely correct, Mustaque-da,' Qadir said. 'Yes, yes—in this heat it is not good for the body or the system . . .'

Qadir kept on talking but Mustaque's attention had already trailed off, his smile disappearing.

'You've got your people ready for the raid on Ghatshila?'

Rahim's head darted up, his eyes alive for a moment. Ghatshila. Raniya's neighbourhood.

Qadir switched effortlessly, 'Yes, I spoke to the boys.'

'Ever since Abdallah's dumbfuck sons swapped over, those piss-drinking fools have been sending down bastards from Meerut. But we've got some more boys from Howrah now along with the others. Brief them by tomorrow, let them know the plan.'

Qadir nodded.

As he wondered what would become of Raniya, Rahim's eyes wandered the room, following the floral design of the thick Iranian carpets, the intricately carved chairs and display cabinets swarming with curios. By now the prospect of becoming a battalion leader had slipped his mind. His thoughts of the girl passed just as easily. He sat mesmerized by the Darjeeling tea boxes adorned with snakes and lotus flowers. The glass sculptures of horses, doves. Beneath them, a collection of silver snuff cases lay sunken in velvet. Sandalwood. Apricot. English rose.

'We have some rifles coming in,' Mustaque said. 'See to the shipment tomorrow night.'

'It's sorted,' Qadir said.

'Coming from Burma. Good maal.'

Two of Mustaque's maids entered the room, a woman carrying a pair of stools, the other a girl holding a tray with two glasses of chilled fresh lime soda. Without a word, Mustaque pointed out where to put down the stools. On seeing Qadir, the girl with the tray hesitated for a moment, then kept walking as if nothing had happened.

'No worries,' Qadir smiled, 'They could be coming from London America—I'll have it sorted the same.'

The woman put down the stools, gestured for Qadir to sit. The girl stood back a moment, the tray in her hands.

'Arrey,' Mustaque chuckled, 'why am I saying Burma? You need to think bigger, my dear Qadir, you need to know the routes. I say Burma because that means the guns will be good. This isn't just any old desi maal from Munger we're talking about.'

When Qadir didn't answer immediately, Rahim turned to look at him. He was staring at the girl holding the tray. It was then that Rahim noticed it was shaking in her hands. Soda spilled over the edge of the glass. For a moment they could see her lips twisting into something, not quite a scowl, nor a false smile. But she bit down on them just as quickly, stopping herself. She was young, but she had the eyes of an older woman, lined and boundless, weighed down by years she'd felt but never seen.

'You're right, Mustaque-da,' Qadir finally said, looking past the girl as he reached out to take the drink. 'You're right. A man needs to know the whole story.'

'There's big trouble out there in Burma now. Great market. Guns and poppies flowing like water.'

The girl finally turned to Rahim, who reached out for the glass. She watched him take it. Her knuckles whitening as she clenched the tray. She was about to say something to him, but stopped. Turned to Mustaque, nodded, asked if she could take her leave.

Mustaque frowned, then, after a moment of consideration, called out to the younger girl, 'Kamala. How could you offer our guests drinks this way? Do it nicely.'

'Sorry.' One of the few words she knew in English.

Mustaque waved her off, but the girl looked at Qadir one last time before she walked away. Lying in the fainting chair, Mustaque spoke of her just loud enough for her to hear him.

'These people,' he said to Qadir, 'they're small-minded. They think they can serve certain people well, then others they treat like this.'

The girl didn't turn around, but her body tightened with each word.

'In this house,' Mustaque went on, 'every guest of mine is equal. Be they Hindu or Muslim. Brahmin or Dalit. Rich or poor.'

Rahim shuffled on his stool.

Qadir nodded, 'You cannot blame them. They don't know, Mustaque-da. Not everyone thinks like you.'

As the men went quiet, Rahim looked up at the deer heads watching them. Their severed necks long and graceful, the antlers leviathan, branching like ancient banyans. A preternatural calm in their glazed resin eyes.

'These I hunted myself,' Mustaque raised his hands, as if to show Rahim the display.

'Your Mustaque-chacha is a fine hunter,' Qadir said.

'One day I'll take you with me. I've heard you've handled some heavy jhamela, let's see how you do with deer.'

'That would be good, Mustaque-chacha.'

'You couldn't use an AK, though. It's not befitting of a sportsman.'

'Yes, Chacha.'

'One day I'll show the sporting rifles. Beautiful British pieces, a hundred years old at least.'

'I would love to see them, Chacha.'

'Just look at him,' Mustaque said to Qadir, ignoring Rahim. 'He really looks like you. It's strange.'

Qadir broke into a big smile.

Mustaque reached out for the armrest of the fainting chair, groaned as he pulled himself up by one hand, the other rubbing his belly under his kurta. He brushed some cigarette ash off his pyjamas and ambled towards Rahim. The boy put his drink down and stood up for him and stayed still without knowing why.

'It's strange, really. Uncanny. He's even built like you were.'

Rahim tensed as Mustaque gripped his bicep, pressed down his arms, as if giving him a massage. The politician's breath was becoming slower, 'Good, good.'

'You're strong. You do gym-fym and all?'

'No, sir.'

'Good, you're too young for it anyhow. There's an age for everything.'

He didn't let go, his hands kept patting down Rahim's body, studying a specimen. Qadir looked on, quietly.

'It's the farming, must be,' Mustaque said, reaching under Rahim's kurta. 'And chest, is it strong?'

His fingers slick with peanut oil, he felt Rahim's chest, his hands moving beneath the thin cotton. Qadir frowned but didn't say anything. Uncertain, Rahim stood still, his smile slowly disappearing as he waited for Mustaque to finish. His eyes gave nothing away, but each breath was laden, animal.

Not knowing what to do, Rahim stared at one of the paintings. Pilgrims wandering the forests.

'Very firm,' Mustaque squeezed Rahim's chest. 'The chest is very important.'

He turned to Qadir, slipping his hands out of Rahim's kurta without the slightest sense of hurry, 'You've got a good boy here.'

As he walked back over and sat down on the fainting chair, they heard a woman's voice across the room.

'Munna,' she screamed, walking in through the drawing-room door. A stout woman with a round, powdered face and oiled hair.

'I'm busy now, darling,' Alam said, lying down.

The woman kept coming towards them. Qadir and Rahim stood up to greet her, but she kept screaming.

'How many times did I tell you,' she said pointing at Qadir, 'I don't want this wicked thing in my house.'

Still lying there, Mustaque clenched his fists as he listened to her.

'We're busy now, my darling,' a harsh whisper. Rahim realized the man's face was trembling with rage.

The woman screamed over him, 'After what he did to that girl, you thought what? To let him into our home.'

'Sir, I should go,' Qadir said, almost begging to leave.

'You stay right there,' Mustaque raised his voice, looked at his wife. 'I told you not to interfere in all this.'

'After what he did to that poor girl, you didn't think for a moment? What? You thought it would be a good idea to let her serve him afternoon snacks?'

Rahim turned to see his father staring down at his feet, his head resting in one hand. Something was rising in his chest, cold and empty.

'Not a snack,' Mustaque's voice was suddenly calm, as if he was trying to negotiate, 'drinks, actually.'

'Bah bah! Idiot. What difference does it make? You brought him to our home? Around my children?'

When he realized he couldn't calm her, Mustaque began shouting himself, 'You be quiet. How dare you?'

'And to make that poor girl serve him. He shouldn't even be in this house. Around my children, my girls.'

For a moment Rahim caught her eye. Her face softened, her voice wavered for a moment, but she kept going. His father whispered his name, but Rahim didn't respond. He didn't want to see Qadir that way.

'You be quiet now. Get the hell out of here.' As Mustaque shouted, his legs seemed to bounce off the seat like a child's. 'You think you can talk to me like that?'

Qadir and Rahim stood quietly as Mustaque and his wife screamed over one another. Catching glances of Qadir from the corner of his eye, it was the first time the boy saw himself in his father, the old man's expression becoming distant, the way Rahim's eyed deadened when his parents fought.

'Feed your dogs elsewhere,' she screamed. 'Not around my children.'

Qadir was wringing his hands, waiting quietly for all of it to pass.

'Not around my kids,' she kept saying over and over again, the end of her sari flailing in the air. 'Not around my daughters. Not around my girls.'

Rahim and Qadir stared ahead as they walked down the garden path towards the bike. The gardeners watched them as they passed by, the maids whispered among themselves, turning away as soon as the boy and his father met their gaze. The smell of diesel and cooking oil permeated the smothering heat. Across the flowerbeds, a cricket bat still lay on the lawn by the wicket stumps. It was almost evening and the game was over. The children had been cleared off the field.

Rahim was about to get on the bike, but Qadir brushed him aside with the back of his hand, swung a rickety leg over the front seat and took hold of the handlebars. Nodded for his son to get on the back. Rahim did as he was told, climbed on and waited, a cacophony bursting in his skull. All he could hear was the woman screaming. His father uttering his name. So much noise in his head that he couldn't feel his thoughts take form.

They went home without a word between them. Qadir drove with his fist tight on the accelerator, his son grabbing his waist. Rahim leaned forward, pressing himself against his father so he wouldn't fall off. As the engine thundered over the sound of the birds, he thought of Mustaque Alam. The politician in his fainting chair. His fingers swarming beneath Rahim's kurta like snakes in a gunny sack.

He recollected how, as they were leaving the mansion, Alam had stopped Qadir at the door, given him a little pat on the cheek, the faintest of smiles. As his father revved the engine, careening down the highway, cranking the dial, he felt lost in the blurred shades of the forest. The leaves drifting past in a pale-green tide.

'Just remember,' the only thing Qadir said as they drove home, 'she eats because of us.'

When Rahim didn't respond, his father turned back and looked him in the eyes, searching.

11

Past the voices, the gunshots, the laughter, the boys took the path through the forest down to the canal, where the sun galvanized the red dirt. Feeling the soil between his toes, Rahim stripped down with the others under the shade of a peepal tree, cleared out a chillum and dived off the ravine's edge into the water. His breath slipped as if into a vacuum, a gasp stolen in the pure, sober cold. He felt a rush as he emerged with his head above the surface and heaved, drunk on dirty air. He could hear the boys calling his name but he didn't listen. He just went under, their screams drowned out beneath the surface, echoing like a distant call to prayer.

He stayed there as long as he could, dragging himself down with both arms. An arc of sunlight burned through the surface, igniting the sunken leaves and the scattered rock, the silver ridges of snakeheads, catlas and long-whiskered catfish slowly flickering around him. He tried not to think of the girl who'd stood there with the tray in her hand. Not much older than him. The other boys plunged in after, lean bodies spearing through the depths, dispersing the colossal mass of industrial dust beneath the water.

Coming up again, Rahim drew in the air, wading slowly. Around him, the boys pulled each other down into the water, kicking and splashing at each other, throwing one another as far as they could. He saw Baltu drag a smaller boy by the neck and clamp him in a headlock, laughing all the while. Seeing them wrestle, he thought of his father. He didn't know why. Qadir sitting on a little step-stool, waiting for the woman to stop screaming.

It was only as Rahim swam away from the other boys that he heard the music. He recognized them before he saw them on the other side of the river, drifted towards them without thinking. The notes were faint in the air. You could see the musicians perched upon the far-off bank in all white, playing old songs, their bare feet cooling among the shoals.

'Ay!' Rahim shouted over to them, raising one hand, but they didn't hear him. He began swimming towards them, cutting through the river to meet the bank. Some of the boys noticed him leave, but didn't say anything.

The music continued across the water. The strings quick and piercing, Amira's voice emanating through heat shimmers, stray wind. Rahim pushed forward with long, hard strokes, the song disappearing as he went under, her voice submerged for moments, drowning in lapses, then rising again with the sound of the trees.

Neither of them acknowledged him when he reached the riverbank. A small clearing, burnt bark and crushed fruit lying beneath the trees. Rahim emerged from the water and walked up the slope, the river pearling on his sleek, dark skin. He walked quietly towards the two musicians. Her eyes closed, Amira sang with her hand raised towards the river, as if to call upon it. As Rahim approached them, he thought he saw her give him a slight nod. He had no way to tell.

Rahim sat down beside her, waiting for the song to end, his chin resting on his fist, an arm slung over one knee. Salim kept his eyes shut as he plucked the dotara, the melody winding down. Leaves scattered around them. Looking out at the water, Rahim could see the boys wrestling on the other side, a morass of limbs in the shade of the banyans and weeping figs.

Salim gradually ceased playing, sighed, then rested the dotara on his lap and watched the still water. Amira reached into her cloth bag for a little sachet of paan masala, slit it open with her rancid, yellow nails.

'How much longer are you two here?'

'We don't know.' Amira slipped the masala into her mouth. 'We got some work. If we keep getting work, what I think is we'll stay a little while longer.'

Rahim paused.

'Didi, don't take this the wrong way. But you shouldn't be out here by yourself.'

When neither responded, Rahim kept talking.

'Stay inside town, don't come out to these places alone. It'll be better for you. For your own good, I'm telling you.'

Amira gave him a tired smile.

'How have you been, Rahim?'

'Fine.' Then, before he was made to speak more about himself: 'What work do you do here?'

'We're singing for a politician,' said Salim, faintly.

'Which one?'

'Ratan Banerjee.'

'He's the MLA,' Rahim said. He'd seen Ratan Banerjee at rallies—a small, portly man with a combover and a clipped moustache, fingers studded with astrological gems.

'Doesn't pay like an MLA,' Amira said.

'But he's a good man,' Salim cut in, 'kind.'

Rahim was the only one laughing.

They saw another figure crossing the river towards them. Baltu, shouting as he swam over, 'Ay, Amira-di, Dada, you remember me?'

Rahim sighed, went quiet as Baltu clambered across the water. Stepping onto the bank, he stood with his hands on his hips, smiling at them.

'So how are you. You recognize me? Got any weed?'

'Just hear who they were playing for,' Rahim said. 'Ratan Banerjee.'

'Ratan Banerjee, oof. You see the inside of his house?'

'That's where we played,' Amira said.

'He's a number one son of a bitch Ratan Banerjee. What's his house like?'

Salim cringed when he heard this.

'Very big.'

Baltu walked over and sat down by Rahim.

'How much you get?' he asked.

'Not much,' said Salim.

Baltu grinned, 'You're being smart. Must have given you more money than you can stash in those big fat jholas of yours.'

Rahim gave him a look, then turned to Amira: 'How long have you two been wandering like this?'

'I don't know,' Amira said, her small sharp teeth stained bright red from the paan. 'I followed some others for a long time. I came up under a guru, but a lot happened there.'

'What happened?'

'I left them.'

'Why?'

Salim spoke up, one hand stroking his beard: 'She didn't like the way it was going—nothing more to it. She thought she could make something by herself.'

Amira cut him off: 'Because he wasn't a real guru.'

'He was no good,' Baltu said. 'I know what you're trying to say.'

Salim furrowed his brow. Amira stared ahead, thinking, *I don't know what he was.*

Rahim saw a red ant on the ground below him. When everyone fell silent, he picked it up in the fold of a tulsi leaf slowly turning his hand so he could watch it run in circles. The breeze stirred, the trees swayed lightly along the banks, bronzed leaves spiralling down into the river like cinders. They could hear the birds bursting from the canopies, shrieking, the beat of their wings thrashing in legion. As the wind came down, it carried the scent of burning dung and white sal-wood char. They could no longer see the boys across the water.

Amira spat onto the edge of the bank, red areca streaking the dark river soil.

'To live under a guru can be a beautiful thing. A seductive thing.'

'That it is,' Salim nodded.

'I've lived under many gurus, musicians, holy men. Witch doctors. Witches.'

'People who could do magic?' Rahim asked.

Amira turned to him, raised an eyebrow, cocked her head askance.

'Real magic.' She went on: 'But magic comes in many forms. When you give yourself to something greater, something beyond yourself, you become a symbol in their language, you see things you didn't see otherwise. It's a spell in itself.'

'Yes,' Salim nodded.

'It makes pilgrims out of drifters. Casts grains of rice into offerings.'

The boys didn't know what she was saying, but while Baltu nodded along, Rahim just stared at the red ant circling the tulsi leaf, listened.

'It starts to bear meaning,' she said. 'It makes the world linear, and you become a part of its language, its future.'

Salim nodded, 'You'll do anything to be carried along with it.'

'Turn blind to the things you can't stop seeing. Forgive the things that can't be forgiven.'

'Because otherwise you're just drifting,' said Salim.

'Because otherwise you're drifting,' Amira repeated, looked at him. 'But if you've given yourself to something, even when you're lost, you know where you're going. You have their language.'

'You have a greater being,' said Salim.

'A greater being you're bound to—you are its speaker and its symbol, the universe twists to their word, you articulate it in their vision.'

'You're talking about God,' Rahim said.

'No. Not God, not always.'

Another gust of wind, this time stronger. On the other side of the river, they could see the boys clearing out, clambering half-naked across the vines draped over the bank.

'When you accept a language, it clarifies certain things, but to illuminate one thing, others must be hidden.'

The boys didn't respond.

'Think of a lens,' Amira said, 'In order sharpen an object, it must blur its surroundings. Truth is nothing but a play of light and shadow.'

Salim considered this as he lit another bidi. Baltu looked at Rahim, trying to make sure he didn't understand either.

'People say a lot of things,' Rahim said.

'What are you talking about, bara?' Baltu slapped him on the shoulder.

'What is it they say?' Salim said.

'They tell us things are good,' Rahim waved off Baltu. 'They tell us things'll only get better.'

'But they stay the same.'

The way the girl had offered Qadir the glass with trembling hands. The way his father had taken it.

Baltu looked at him out the corner of his eye, grinned.

'And why do you listen to them?' Salim asked.

Baltu rubbed his fingers together, 'Cash, dada. Cash. What else?'

'You're not a foolish boy, Rahim,' Salim said. 'Tell me really.'

Rahim hesitated.

'And me?' Baltu asked, with a hand to his heart. 'Am I foolish?'

Rahim watched the ant move on the tulsi leaf, running over its edge only to re-emerge along the other side, caught in an endless revolution. He thought of the woman in the living room. A young girl encircled in a chamber of stuffed heads, staring down at Qadir on his little step-stool, fresh lime soda pooling in the aluminium tray.

Rahim didn't know why but was beginning to feel light-headed, this emptiness deep in his gut, his feet going numb under his weight. When he looked around, he could see the others watching him. They were talking, but he couldn't make out the words. A part of him felt if he reached out, his hand would go right through them. He could steal their faces and rearrange them like masks in a beggars' theatre.

'So why do you do it, babu?' Salim said, 'Why do you listen to them?'

Baltu looked Rahim in the eye, 'Because you don't want to starve.'

Amira muttered, 'Because you don't want to be alone.'

The ant turned to run the other way but nothing happened. It was still there. The burning homes, the mourners' prayers, bodies left in gunny sacks along the highway. Skinned and half-buried in the jungle, crawling out of the dirt like night crawlers. He saw it all now. He was still young, but a part of him knew something had already been stolen.

Rahim tossed the leaf into the river, slung an arm over one knee like his father.

'I'll never be alone,' he said.

12

The day before a raid, Rahim's mother would make certain the boys prayed before the last meal. She cleaned the younger ones with her own hands. Then, kneeling, they touched their heads upon the carpets, madurkathi and cane woven into depictions of the mihrab. Visions laid out on the floor like a fractal metropolis. Cities of looming domes and smooth, black monoliths.

The boys followed Qadir, the old man muttering under his breath, his palms raised in this theatre of exaltation. Rahim watched from the corner of his eye, grimacing. He could not tell you now how much of this was mimicry. A play of shadows emerging from the passage to God's light, angels through the looking glass. The spider's lips uttering the faintest echoes of the Lord's word, his glory, the distortion of hallowed forms.

They ate a late lunch on the floor. The family gathered around stainless-steel plates of fried fish laid upon mounds of panta rice, the edges lined with dried chillies, raw onions, ash gourd and salt. Charred hunks of slow-cooked beef for Rahim and his father. There were two AKs laid side by side on the floor beyond them, above a row of magazines. Machetes were wrapped in butcher rolls and newspaper. A rusted, desi grenade launcher leaned against the wall like a crude flower vase.

It was Friday, and Qadir was in his prayer clothes. A pale-green, synthetic-silk kurta. His bright taqiyah adorned in a constellation of roses and crescent moons. When he asked Rahim if he'd cleaned the 9 mm's, the boy told him yes, but didn't look up from his food. The old man paused for a moment, then moved on. This is how it had been these past few days. A series of desultory nods, vague gestures, perhaps a flick of the wrist as his sentences trailed into nothing.

He'd seen the way Qadir looked at him in these moments, the flashes of rage in his eyes dying in a moment of hesitation, regret. It was the same thing. They turned away from each other, continued eating. The food tasteless these few days. Like cud.

The boy knew not to take it further. His head bowed, trying not to catch his fathers' eye, he thought of Mustaque Alam, and suddenly he wasn't so hungry. When his mother tried to ladle more rice onto his plate, he put up a hand to stop her.

'What's wrong?'

'I'm full.'

'What are you saying?'

'I won't have any more. I'm full.'

Qadir watched him, weighing his words. In response Rahim took the hunks of beef off his plate and doled them out to his younger brothers.

‘What are you doing?’ His mother nearly gasped.

‘I can’t eat any more.’ Rahim said, looking at his father. His lips verging on a scowl.

‘Accha,’ Qadir nodded slowly. ‘I see.’

He waved Rahim off with one hand.

‘Are you crazy? Tell your son to eat. He’ll fall sick.’

‘I don’t know,’ Qadir grunted. ‘He’s a man now, I suppose.’

Rahim stood up to wash his hands.

‘He’s a man so he knows everything. Isn’t that right, Rahim?’ Qadir went on.

‘Say something,’ Rahim’s mother implored.

‘Rahim, isn’t that right?’

‘Are you crazy?’ Rahim’s mother grabbed the beef off her younger sons’ palates.

Rahim made his way outside, his mother following him with handfuls of beef and rice, telling him he’d get sick as she tried to shove the food into his mouth. The eldest child kept walking, as if he hadn’t even noticed. His father shook his head. Took the taqiyah off, dropped it on his lap and continued eating. The younger boys looked at each other, trying not to laugh.

13

They did their last field drills on the dawn of the raid. Forty boys crawling backwards in the dirt side by side, a long bamboo rod under the crook of one arm of each, their blackened heels tearing through the grass. Rahim was ahead of the others, twisting with the grace of a river eel as he moved towards the boundary line, where Qadir stood over them shouting orders.

It had been days now since he'd spoken to his father. Racing towards the far side of the pitch, he could see Qadir looking down at him. A lapse in the practised glare. Rahim turned and began crawling the other way, staring up at the grey sky as he scrambled through the field, convinced his father was still watching him.

They worked all through the morning, the barefoot swarm breaking into battalions, rehearsing ambushes and guerrilla formations passed down by the Maoists, taking turns to play dead as their comrades carried them across the field. Qadir paced the edges. His voice harsh with smoke and rising acid, yelling for them to go harder, past the suffocation, the sinking numbness. This is how we'll bury you.

Rahim ran with Baltu on his back, head bowed as he kept pushing forward, his heart beating like it was trying to break out of his chest. The older boy hung on his back like dead weight, talking incessantly.

'You been eating the guavas my mother sent?'

Rahim panting as he drove his legs forward.

'The guavas are coming out great this year.'

'Shut up, na.'

'Bhai, they're completely pink inside. I couldn't believe it myself.'

When they made it to the boundary line, Rahim put Baltu down and lay in the grass, his turn to lay still.

Baltu crouched and hoisted him onto his shoulders, began running towards the other side. Rahim hung over the older boy's back, his body limp, waiting as he was carried towards his father. He tried to keep still but he needed to run again. He needed to break himself down until he was submerged. The rush of wind and blood swallowing the voices in his head.

But he hung on a while longer. Waited his turn. A breeze drifted past, the air cool and still. He rested his head against Baltu's back, he could feel his dead in the smell of the older boy's bleeding sores. He knew they would keep coming, so he stayed calm. This was usually how they found him. His ghosts were imprisoned in the musk of gunpowder, tulsi soap and poppies, in the scent of the tall grass after rain.

It came from the smell of young flesh. A memory of December emerging, the third kill he'd collected out in the field. Another rapist, Qadir had said. Another dacoit. Rahim didn't want to think of it, but as he pushed forward, the warm grass curling against his bare soles, a part of him conjured the man's face, dragging this corpse out from the recesses of his mind.

They trudged across the grass. This broken formation. A death march in silent pantomime. As they reached the other side, Rahim took Baltu over his shoulders once more, the older boy's breath now worn and shallow. The bodies gradually reanimating at the boundary line, the boys arched their backs, swung their necks like hounds and shook their bones into order, rising to take the place of the living.

Rahim could feel his legs slipping, giving away under him, but all he knew was to just go faster. As he heard his father's voice bellowing over the others, he couldn't stop thinking of December. A job out in Howrah. Qadir strangling the man from behind with jute rope, his crooked legs wrapped around the mark's waist, as though a langur cradling her child in her lap.

Rahim grunted through it, setting his weight down, forcing himself to feel all of it. He knew not to take a moment, not to let himself breathe. His father had once told him not to trust the calm. Death breeds in silence. There is no promise crueller than reprieve. As he felt his muscles burn, he thought of Qadir holding the mark down from behind, choking him only enough to keep him still without killing him, shouting for Rahim to grab the brick and smash it between those flailing legs.

The boy had listened, of course. Even now, as he ran, exhaustion blurring his senses, he could hear the mark's screams as he'd brought the brick down, grinding it into the man's loins. Rahim had done it again, then again. Warm and then cold. An entanglement of thin, macerated skin and crushed vessels beneath him. Nothing left in the end but a chasm. A flowering womb. He could hear his father's voice howling for him to keep going, and he did.

He ran, a phantom ache throbbing between his own legs, an emptiness rising through his body. He made his way through the field, lay Baltu down, then dropped to the ground, waited. The same vision of limp, gelded bodies lying side by side in the poppy fields, their skin washed smooth and bloodless with sulphur, watching the clouds pass overhead with black marble eyes.

Loosening his muscles, Rahim let himself hang, his breath becoming slow. He played dead again. Watching the grassland stretch away from him like a river. His father's voice becoming soft and flyaway as the older boy carried him forward. The cold ache under his waist. The distant paddies a strange, spectral blue beneath the pale dawn light.

14

That night their battalion gathered along the edges of Berapur with the other men—mercenaries streaming into the arms units along the remnants of an abandoned sponge-iron mill. They kept coming through, dozens of them arriving in disparate hordes—SUVs and biker tribes, anthems blasting from the backs of their jeeps. *Khela Hobe. Goli Maar. Electric Piya.* Disco beats pulsing and dissonant among the dark swathe of banyans and gnarled sals. They drove through the clearings in the jungle. The barren stretches of industrial waste, rusted cogs and gearwheels half-buried in the ash and dust, scattered like relics across a desolate inland sea.

Men stood on the beds of construction trucks, pounding their fists on the roofs to the beat of the music. The dispossessed emerging from the slums of Kanpur, Dhanbad and Howrah. The ex-cons, the addicts. Street kids from Calcutta hawking souls over benzos and satta debts. Then the older, quieter ones. The veterans. Ragged foot soldiers draped in ammo belts, fruit-stone beads and pig-iron chest plates, others in khakis and distressed Russian Kevlar, notches carved into their rifles, tribal etchings. The fugitive cadres of dacoit clans and shattered revolutions. The drifting gunmen transient, resolute, careening from void to void like wind-up ghouls.

Rahim and Baltu walked among the growing crowd in short shorts and bulletproof vests over their Chelsea jerseys. A sub-machine gun cradled in the younger boy's arms, he gnawed at a cold sore the way cinema dons chewed paan. While passing the arms units, he could hear the rhythmic clack of rifles loading, white lashes of chillum smoke sweeping out of the doorways. Electronica blasting from the dusty, bootleg speakers of the boy shooters, screaming and discordant, like creatures in a burning forest. Amidst all this, the muted undertones of whispered prayers. The final calls home. A claustrophobia sinking in as Rahim shoved through the crowds.

Over the men's shoulders, he could see Qadir. His father holding a congregation before a fleet of motorcycles. His rifle in one hand, he stroked his long, white beard with the other. Body armour slung over his shirt. His lungi held up by a calfskin ammo belt, two 9 mm's tucked down the front.

Pacing back and forth in his wild shamble, Qadir shouted out to them.

'These people swapped over when times were tough, and we know what'll happen,' he said, his fingers clawing through his beard, 'Don't we?'

The men nodded, shouted in response. Rahim felt his body turning hot. Beside him, Baltu cupped his hands around his mouth and howled before popping another pill.

'They taunted us, didn't they? They fucked their own people in the ass. Told us what would happen to our women, our children.'

As the men cheered, Qadir raised one hand, nodding slowly.

'And now what? Now what do they expect? What were the promises they made us? Nothing. So this is what I promise them.'

The men cheered as he went on, telling them to empty the streets and bomb out the houses. Leave it all barren, he said. These people were tainted. The children of rape. Then, with a strange sidelong grin that made them quiet, he told them to make certain there would be no burials—you will hollow their rooms of breeders, descendants—the whispers of blood oaths and mourning. Bring the world under your order, he said, scatter them across the forest like cinders, foster a tribe of exiles and ghosts.

'Do you understand me?' he asked, his voice low but resonant, a hand to his heart, 'Do you understand?'

The men cheered, their rifles in the air. Hearing them, Rahim began to feel the old rush, but even then he didn't raise his gun with the others. He could see the men passing bidis and downing bottles of bangla, pouring it into the mouths of those besides them, moonshine spilling down their necks and soaking their shirts. Baltu shaking his bony hips beneath the pale cascades of rising smoke.

He heard the music swell, the cadres singing with the speakers slung over their shoulders. All of them chanting along to it, 'Khela hobe. Khela hobe.'

Seeing his father on the podium, godlike, a nightmare drifting above the men's shoulders, Rahim could feel the bareness in his stomach dissipating. The nausea momentarily subsiding to elation, a pride he could no longer tell apart from love.

Then, without thinking, he began shouting with the others. His voice a low rumble he couldn't recognize. The chant emerging from deep inside his gut. A possession of the bones. He cheered along and embraced Baltu as the swarming bodies closed in. The hot stink of moonshine, sulphur and tobacco permeating from the collective mass.

Before the thoughts could start crowding him again, he turned to the man beside him and asked for a pull of whiskey. The man looked him up and down. This tall, emaciated Northerner with a greying stubble and eyes shot through with jaundice.

'Can I have some, bhaiya?' Rahim asked in broken Hindi. In a way he already felt half-drunk, but he knew it wouldn't last unless he had something real.

'Come, bhai, na?'

The man gave him an uncertain smile. They both realized Qadir was standing over them, watching. When Rahim felt the thoughts crowding in again, he asked the man once more. When the Northerner nodded, the boy grabbed the neck of the bottle from his hand and downed it, the whiskey lukewarm and rancid, scouring out the voices like strychnine.

The man was trying to say something, but Rahim ignored him.

'Ay ay, don't finish it all.'

Looking out for Qadir, even Baltu was uncertain now, his smile a little uneasy.

The Northerner grabbed the bottle back when he saw it being half-emptied. Before he could shout, Rahim had already begun dancing, pretending it had hit him. He bit down on his lip and kept going, pulling off this little three-step jig with the SMG tucked under his arm. He knew his father was watching him, but he embodied the moment now, revelled in it.

He figured he could will himself out of his shame. The memory of his father, head bowed, waiting for the screaming to stop. The Alam women stood over him. The girl out of time. An offering in her hands, her eyes chasmic, deadening. He could feel it gone now with the passing bliss, Amira's voice drowned out in the babel. Blindness, he remembered. That's what the musicians had said. He could feel Qadir's eyes following him from across the crowd, but it didn't matter. All he could do now was dance, aping the men around him, possessed by the human tide. There was a warmth in this, he realized now. A comfort. Four hundred thousand years in waiting.

15

Perhaps, one day when Rahim was older, he would think again about the way they lived. The way they held their children, the way they ate, laughed and slept—it was as though they could transpire at will, their souls slipping from their bodies like a soft, winter breath while they culled the fields.

It could be he considered this, or it could be he would come to the same conclusion as his father. They never truly disappeared. In these moments of slaughter, it was not alien blood running through their veins but their own. Nothing was altered. These were the same, ruined hands that fed their sons, their daughters. The same eyes that watched the river pass in quiet moments. The same bodies drawn crying from the wombs.

Yet, as the boy walked along the fringes of Ghatshila with the gun in his hands, firing into the distance, all he could think about was the figures along the horizon, his thoughts veering between boredom and euphoria. When he was certain he killed a man, the world was electric. The colours bright and vivid, like the forest after rain. In the waiting moments, hiding from gunfire, firing into the distance was muted and listless. This lingering, prosaic sense of dread that followed you home from the field.

Even then, a part of him knew these moments would be bred into him. His dead would scream in the lapse of each heartbeat. In the nights, when he lay down to sleep, he would see a white blindness flare across the ringing silence and pure, jungle dark like the death of stars.

It was always with him, he'd just learned not to utter it. Not to let it form into words. It was the way he could keep walking along the fringes, firing at anything that moved in the distance—his body glazed in dusk, blood and sweat, the gun singeing the skin of his palms as he cut down the glimpses of saffron and shadows, watching the bodies fall.

They'd been fighting for hours now and it was coming to dawn. The anti-party gunmen were beginning to run, leaving the villagers behind. Those who surrendered were killed where they stood. Bullets cut through the air, but Rahim told himself he was giddy with spirits and adrenaline and the world was coming to him so easy. He saw skulls burst open in the periphery of his vision and grit his teeth, the blood streaking across the dried dung walls.

From across the village, he could see hear Alam's men bombing out the homes. They circled the rivals' fields on motorcycles lobbing petrol bombs at the poppies, their swords raised in the air as the flowerheads swayed at the impact, unreal sweeps of white swarmed and darkened in the flames.

On the other side, their battalions butchered the surrendered gunmen. Men with their hands clasped, begging in myriad tongues. His father's men dragged the women and children out into the dirt and beheaded them where they kneeled. Qadir looked over this in silence, his hand gently brushing the rifle slung over his shoulder, keeping it in place the way you would calm an animal. As he stood there in the tall grass, the fire in the poppy fields wreathed above his shoulders. His eyes passing through his son. Nothing more.

Rahim turned away, wiped the sweat off his brow and began firing once more at the distant houses. Beyond the gunfire and muted screams, he could just about hear someone call his name. Baltu's voice. Rahim turned to see him standing with a dozen other village boys, a pack of them barefoot in the sedge, red-eyed and shuddering with the amphetamines.

'Come here, bara,' Baltu shouted, waving him over. Rahim could barely hear him, but he read the boy's lips and followed, the musk of poppies and nitroglycerin curdling the thick, mossy air like rotten fruit. Saccharine and burning.

Baltu kept shouting and Rahim pretended to listen, his shoulders swinging as he followed the boys towards the remaining huts. They marched through the narrows of the village, burning thatch and charred furniture was scattered by the open sewers, cattle lying dead and tethered in the streets by the bodies of anti-party cadres. Rahim's eyes lingered on the half-naked child lying spread-eagled beside them, a bullet hole smoking from his forehead. An onyx third-eye.

'That bitch's house is out here somewhere,' Baltu said.

'Who?' Rahim asked, though he already knew the answer.

The boys broke into groups, some sprinting ahead to do sweeps on the houses, begging and gunfire emerging from the doorways. When an anti-party man burst out from one of the houses, firing blindly with an AK, the boys cut him down right there in the street, ripping him apart as he staggered and gasped before collapsing onto the pile of bodies. They realized one of theirs had died too, but they kept moving, stepping over the corpses. Old men. Mothers and their children. The women's pale, bloodstained shawls blowing down the gullies like tainted petals.

Baltu led Rahim and five other boys to the end of the lane, where a corner shop had been blown up with a grenade launcher. Breadcrumbs and shattered Thums Up bottles lay in the rubble, cola pooling into milk and blood like lacquer. Baltu gave a nod as they approached one of the houses, a rundown hut with a rusted tin roof and a curtain over the entrance, the clay walls studded with lead. The two boys took position on either side of the doorway, their guns ready. Amidst the droning gunfire, Rahim looked at Baltu, nodded, then swept the curtain aside and stormed in together.

The family was huddled together in one corner. The mother with her arms around the crying children. Raniya among them. Sobbing, the girl shielded her brothers with her arms, one hand clasped over a little boy's eyes.

'Your brother's dead,' Baltu said, slowly walking towards them. 'Your father too.'

Rahim could see the women's lips moving, but he just stood in the doorway, his gun trained on the family. Sunlight streamed through the bullet holes, white specks across the small, bare room. Nothing more than a gas cylinder and a cooker in one corner. Children's toys strewn across the mattress where they used to sleep.

As Baltu closed in on them, the family pressed against the wall, holding their children closer. Grinning, Baltu clutched Raniya by the hair and dragged her towards them, throwing her across the room at Rahim's feet. As the mother screamed and reached out for her, Baltu fired, watching each of them fall like marionettes cut from their strings, a mass of asbestos clay dust rising over their bodies. For a few moments, he stared at them with a far-off, abstracted gaze, then fired another burst when he saw the little boy squirming beneath his mother's body.

He turned to look at Raniya, the girl screaming, tears running down her face. When she tried to scramble up and run, Rahim pushed her back. Baltu took a step forward and kicked her in the head, watched her lurch and stumble to the side, one hand grabbing her head as she wheezed, the other raised as if it could stop them. Lowering their guns, the boys approached her slowly.

'Come on, hero,' Baltu said, smiling at Rahim. 'I'll let you go first. I've already had her.'

When she heard this, the girl's cries softened, if only for a moment. She looked up at the boys with a hint of a preternatural detachment, as though she already knew what she was resigned to. As though it had happened before. When she began again, she screamed, but didn't beg. She knew there was no use.

Rahim forced a smile, then turned to the girl. He didn't feel anything as he crawled on top of her thrashing body. He was still cold to her. To keep her still, he grabbed her by the hair and punched her, hitting her again and again, one hand reaching down his shorts, trying to feel something.

Baltu stood there, waiting. It was just the three of them now. Kids, really. Their bodies sleek with blood. Skin dusted in the white chemical mist. The sound of grenades filled the skies like an all-consuming storm.

'Come on,' Baltu said. 'Just fuck her already.'

Rahim pinned her neck down with one hand. His other working furiously to make himself hard. Nothing. He could feel the old sickness rising in him. As his thoughts slowly returned, her screams ripped through his skull and his crowding thoughts. Hitting her one more time, he remembered about the things they'd said about his father. The women who'd followed him. The way he'd slip poppies into their hair. Rahim didn't believe it now. Another fable, he thought. Another ghost story.

'Do it quick,' Baltu said. 'Before the others come.'

Her hair was falling over her face, sticking to the blood, mucus and tears. Blood was gushing from her nose. Her cheekbones were shattered. She clutched his shirt, trying to push him away, but he could feel her fading beneath him, passing in and out of consciousness as his hand wriggled under his pants.

He tried masturbating like it would keep him alive, but there was no use. He was limp. She was broken, but he couldn't have her. When her breathing calmed for a moment, he panicked even more, his rage withering into fear. He grabbed her by the hair and dragged her closer.

'What are you doing?' Baltu said. 'Just have a go. Or let me go.'

As the older boy shouted at him, Rahim could feel his chest hollowing out. The girl averted his eyes. He could feel this sinking dread, like dying.

'All right, get off her, we don't have time.'

'No, wait.'

'Give me a go.'

'Wait,' Rahim looked up at him, growling.

'Let me have a go, before the others come.'

Rahim pulled up his shorts with one hand, raised the gun with the other and shot Raniya in the head. Just like that. Her surging blood warm on his skin.

'What the fuck did you do?' Baltu shouted.

Rahim shook his head, spat on the floor and walked out of the hut into the burning streets, making sure he didn't have to look at her. Baltu trailed behind him, shouting.

'You could've just given me a shot at her, bara,' he said. 'Selfish fucker.'

Rahim kept walking down the lane, where the boys had brought survivors to watch them dismember the dead, the blood staining their synthetic sports jerseys. He picked up a sword from a dead cadre's body and began to play with another one of the corpses. Baltu shouted from behind, but Rahim stood in the narrows hacking at the body of a gunman, the rubble and scraps of charred newspaper at his feet. Recollecting the way the girl's eyes had glazed over, buried in time, he slashed open the man's stomach, dragging out fistfuls of his intestines—displacing one insanity for another.

By now dawn had passed. It was hot, and he could feel Raniya's blood drying on his face. Organs lay scattered in the streets beneath a bright blue sky. Human offal, slick and grey like beached sea creatures. The small, headless bodies of children. A man lying with his chest ripped open, the entrails blood ripe and flowering, tethering his ribcage like vines.

For a moment he hesitated, looked up towards the horizon for his father, as though searching for some order in all of this—for reason. He watched the other boys walking amid this, moving from body to body, working with the mindless determination of farmers, leaving the corpses behind like ploughed fields. He took breaks, still glancing up at the horizon every few moments, but all he could see were the fires spreading along the poppy fields. He looked for the longest time.

16

The last time Rahim saw the musicians, they were leaving for the railway station. He was heading back from town on his bicycle. Salim and Amira walking through the small jungle path towards him, broken bushels of fruit spilling from their jholas, lychees and tamarind pods dangling like little temple bells. It was downhill for him and he was moving fast enough that he could have just passed them by. It was something he did consider, even as the words were on the tip of his lips, 'Oh, Didi, Dada, where are you going?'

Amira smiled when she saw him, 'To the train station.'

Rahim slowed the bike as he approached them, made a stop and leaned over the handles as he spoke, resenting them for crossing his path, making him talk when he barely had a word for anyone.

'You're leaving?'

'For Birbhum,' she said. 'We have a performance.'

They all stepped aside to let an old man pass on his scooter. As the sound of the engine disappeared, birdcalls seemed to emerge from the leaves, sharp and perfectly clear.

Rahim nodded, then gestured to the fruit with a nod, 'And that?'

'Ratan-da gave them to us,' Salim said.

'He's Ratan-*da* now?'

Amira laughed, plucking lychees and tamarind pods from the stalks.

Salim turned away for a moment, lit a bidi to hide his pained smile. Amira passed a lychee to Rahim before she began carving through one for herself with her nails.

'Did he finally pay you?' Rahim asked. His voice different today, an edge to it, as if stripped of its boyhood, its deference.

'He did,' Amira said. 'He took us around town in his car, around his orchard. How beautiful it was.'

'It must have been very beautiful,' Rahim said as he ripped the fruit open with his teeth and sunk into its pulp and reddened skin, the flesh ripe and faintly boozy. Oversweet.

'He's a good man from what I understood,' Salim said. 'Not like the others.'

'Oh, is he?' Rahim said, sucking on the fruit.

Taken aback, Salim hesitated for a moment before Amira stepped in.

'What Salim means is, we spoke to some of the villagers. They said he's done a lot for the people around here. The water situation and whatnot. Roads. Education.'

'I see,' Rahim smirked without pleasure, teasing them, drawing out the uncertainty. 'So he helps a lot of people, is that right? I guess you could say that.'

Rahim tossed the peel onto a pile of charred trash on the roadside.

'They said there's been a lot of development.'

'Who said?'

'The villagers.'

'Yeah, that's what they'll say.'

'You don't seem to think so,' Amira said, scraping at the tamarind with her teeth, its deep, blood-red pulp collecting against the edge of her teeth like the milk of the poppy.

Rahim paused, considered this for a moment.

'You didn't hear about what happened on Monday, did you?'

'No, what happened?'

Rahim hesitated, his eyes darting between them. When he spoke, it was in a deadpan.

'You don't know about Ghatshila?'

'No.'

'All those people his men killed, you didn't hear that? It's close by.'

When they didn't respond, Rahim kept going, 'Women. Children. They didn't leave anyone.'

'What are you saying?' Amira stopped eating and stared at the boy.

'That's it, that's what I'm saying. So what good work has he done?'

The musicians looked at each other. Long silences swept between the bird songs. As the clouds passed over, the leaves seemed to pale and darken. The jungle seemed to sway overhead with a soft, demonic hum.

'Who told you that?' Salim turned to Rahim, frowning, an eyebrow raised. 'We didn't hear anything like that.'

'Dada, you've travelled a lot, haven't you?'

'Yes.'

'You've been to many places, met many people. You know more than me.'

Salim accepted this.

'So,' the boy said, 'we're all blind, isn't that what you said?'

'But the police . . . If what you're saying is true, they need to look into this. They need to investigate.'

'They know,' Rahim said. 'They're with us.'

He turned to Amira, his stare boring into her, making her take half a step back. Between the long pauses, he glared at them, as if waiting for a response—a test, perhaps, an invocation. Traces of Qadir in his gaze.

'And people in media?' Salim went on.

'They're with us too,' Rahim laughed, then said to Amira, 'What, Didi? Am I saying anything wrong?'

Amira hesitated, her hand instinctively brushed her shawl to the side. Salim sucked on his bidi in quick, uneasy sips, barely breathing the smoke in, just waiting for the moment to pass.

'We should go, Rahim,' Amira said.

The boy shifted in his seat, gripped the handles of the bicycle, 'All right.'

After a while, Amira looked at the boy, tried to smile, 'Take some lychee, some tamarind.'

She brought out a bushel of each and passed them to Rahim. The boy took them quietly, rested the branches between the handlebars.

'You best keep well, babu,' Amira said, stood there uncertain, as if a part of her was still convinced this was a child, that she could at least put her hand upon his—but she didn't.

She just kept walking down the narrow road, Salim following close behind her. Before leaving, Rahim almost called for them, wondering if he'd give them one last smile, make them laugh, knowing this wasn't how he wanted them to remember him. He didn't say anything. He just went home.

17

On Friday, Rahim sat on the floor with his mother, scrolling through his father's phone as she ate rabri off a steel plate. After the raid, Alam had sent sweets and dried fruit to the homes of all the gunmen. Candy-red parcels of rosogolla, langcha and dates. Little milk cakes burnt golden with syrup, dark pools of ghee soaking through the cardboard.

Rahim, one chillum down, was watching clips of some girl lip-syncing love songs. *Aami tomaro songe* . . . His mother had laid out a plate of rabri for him too, but he hadn't touched a thing.

'Eat,' she told him.

'I will,' he said, taking a handful of rabri and licking it off his fingers, crushed pistachios and thick kheer. He couldn't tell, it could have been anything. The faintest aftertaste of ash.

'It's good, isn't it?'

'Yes.'

'Not too sweet.'

For a while now, he'd barely touched food. His mother had thought it was a fever, but when she pressed the back of her hand on his forehead, it was nothing. Cold. These past few days, his nausea had curled up like a parasite, an unborn child inside him, feeding on his hunger. When he recalled the way Raniya cried, he could see her face, her eyes. A girl on his phone mouthed the words *only you* and touched both hands to her heart.

'Eat more.'

Rahim grunted, thinking about the raid again. Recollecting moments he hadn't considered when he stood over the girl, punching her with one hand, the other down his pants. She'd been in a blue shawl.

'You don't eat like you used to.'

The same blue shawl she'd worn in the picture Baltu had first shown him, telling him she would give it up, she was theirs.

When Rahim did not respond, his mother said, 'Eat. You'll become weak.'

He looked up at her, not really listening.

She took a handful of rabri and put it into his mouth, feeding him. He ate it off her fingers while staring at the phone, scrolling through the clips. Love songs. Choreographed fights. A girl pushing a boy, slapping him, dragging him back as he begins hitting himself. As he watched, he thought of Raniya when they'd first entered her home. The way her eyes had lit up. He hadn't realized it then, but she'd been relieved to see Baltu. A boy she'd once known.

'I'd told your father not to take you out there,' his mother cleaned her plate off. 'I told him to wait a few years, when you're older.'

'It's not that,' he said, putting the phone aside.

'That's all it is.'

'Whatever's out there, I can handle it.'

'Of course you can, babu,' she said, setting her plate down. It was shining. No trace of cream.

'Baba was even younger when he started.'

'You've got everything from your father—his face, his eyes, his hands. But you're not like your brothers. You think like me.'

She reached out and touched his face. 'You know, you'll hear it from everyone, they'll say the world is going bad, you can't trust anyone. You'll think it too, one day. But it's not that.' She turned Rahim's face towards hers, making him look her in the eyes, and continued, 'Everyday they find a new reason to tell you the world is coming to an end.'

Rahim saw Raniya on the floor, waiting for him.

'But that's not it,' his mother placed her hand on his. 'It's just that they were raised with promises, and those promises are being broken now. It isn't the world ending. It's just a little part of you being taken away.'

'You figure out none of it was true.'

'It was all true in a way. They were not lies, babu. Just promises we thought we could keep.'

'I can handle it.'

She took his plate, fed him another mouthful of rabri.

'Whatever it is, just remember, your father loves you. It's all that matters.'

For a moment, Rahim almost told her about Raniya. What he'd done to her. Just to see something change in his mother's eyes.

The words didn't come, but for a moment he thought they didn't need to. She knew.

'Whatever he's done, it doesn't make his love for you any less. I realized this a long time ago. He is your father and that's all that matters.'

Her body relaxing, she removed her hand from his, smiled in a way he'd never seen before, as though she'd become an older form of herself, blurring the confines of the small asbestos hut, slipping out of time into something he couldn't recognize.

'Love isn't easy to find, so take it when you can. It doesn't matter.' She looked around and whispered as if it were a secret, 'If it's the truth you're looking for, you'll always be restless. Sweet things are never honest.'

Then, when she was done, it was as though the room closed in on them. Her smile disappeared. She got on her haunches and slowly began closing the sweet boxes with her clean hand.

'Go help your father,' she said.

18

As Rahim stepped outside, he could hear his brothers calling to him. They were crouching in the paddies with their father. Qadir, with a sickle in one hand, trudging through the field like a hexed scarecrow, the sun scalding his back as he worked the fields, hacking at the pale-gold stalks of rice with the blade.

Taking another sickle from the iron slab backed against the wall, he went to join them, his mother hunched by the cooker, watching him from the open doorway. As he walked into the fields, his father raised his head in acknowledgment, nodded. Rahim crouched in the paddy, taking strands of the rice plants in one hand before sweeping them with his sickle, tearing their roots from the sun-baked dirt like fistfuls of human hair. It almost made him flinch.

When Rahim looked up, he could see his father ahead of him. Qadir shuffling forth on his crooked legs, moving quickly through the paddy, his light-red lungi fringed with dirt. The plants towering over his small, curled body. Rahim began working faster, closing in on him, his legs shredded by the rice stubble. The blood thick and sticky. Warm syrup.

They moved forward on their haunches, tossing the butchered stalks back over their shoulders. As they worked, the heat flickered along the edges of the horizon, softening the division between the fields and the sky beyond them, bearing down on their breath and the passage of time. They moved slowly. Lean bodies. Clockwork shadows drawing the barren swathes of gold. Their deep blue, corded veins tensing over the blade handles, loosening like industrial chains.

When the breeze blew, long and solitary, Rahim looked up to see the paddies stirring beyond him. For a moment he almost stopped. He almost dropped the sickle to lie down in the clearing for a few moments, waiting for the breeze to come over him like water—but he kept working, the muscles knotting in his bent legs. In a way he hoped it would stop blowing, but it didn't. It only gathered. The cool air slipped through the plants. A storm of stray leaves and petals skimmed over the swaying stalks.

Still, he moved forward, reaping. He told himself it wouldn't last. When he wavered, it was only for a moment, as he caught a glimpse of his father stooped over across the field. After a few moments Qadir stood up and turned to face the wind, the sun mirrored upon his chest.

When Rahim finally stopped and faced his father, he saw him lingering. Qadir's body a blade's edge against the vast expanse of gold. As Rahim stopped, letting the breeze pass over, he found himself looking at his father's old gunshot wound. The bullet the

Spider still kept in his belly for luck, it was said. When Qadir closed his eyes, breathed in, Rahim dropped his sickle and watched. His eyes drawn to scar. Looking at the skin coil around it, slowly distorting in the heat shimmer, twisting like a vortex in dark waters. Rahim watched as his father exhaled and put one hand out to the wind, his fingers grazing the rush of stray leaves.